One Night
with the CEO

One Night with the CEO

MIA SOSA

New York   Boston

Forever Yours
Hachette Book Group
1290 Avenue of the Americas
New York, NY 10104
hachettebookgroup.com
twitter.com/foreverromance

First edition: May 2016

Forever Yours is an imprint of Grand Central Publishing.
The Forever Yours name and logo are trademarks of Hachette Book Group, Inc.

The Hachette Speakers Bureau provides a wide range of authors for speaking events. To find out more, go to www.hachettespeakersbureau.com or call (866) 376-6591.

The publisher is not responsible for websites (or their content) that are not owned by the publisher.

ISBN: 978-1-4555-6844-4 (ebook), 978-1-4555-6842-0 (print on demand

For Anika

Acknowledgments

I'm in awe of the many writers in the romance industry who continually elevate their craft and write stories that touch our hearts, stretch our minds, make us laugh, and inspire us to get our sexy on (ahem). You all deserve a slow clap, a standing ovation, and a fist bump. Thank you for showing me how it's done.

Speaking of how it's done, Dana Hamilton is an editor extraordinaire, y'all. I went through some dark writing moments to get this book in readers' hands. Dana helped me to see the light, and she did so with kindness. Instead of asking, "What is this crap?" Dana told me "This needs work," and then she helped me tell a better story. I can't thank you enough for your guidance, Dana. (Insert dancing baby gif here.)

My new editor, Madeleine Colavita, has confirmed what I'd already suspected: The team at Grand Central is awesome. Thank you for being gracious and helpful, Madeleine. I'm looking forward to working with you!

My agent, Sarah Younger, deserves many kudos, too. She helps to keep me centered—a significant task, I assure you—and she gives me more brilliant advice in a single phone call than any person should reasonably expect to receive in a lifetime. I'm so lucky to have you in my corner, Sarah.

My friend and critique partner, Olivia Dade, has helped me to become a better writer *and* a better friend. We've stumbled through this writing journey together, and there's no other writer I'd rather stumble with. Olivia, our long phone calls, sprints, and writing sessions fuel my creativity and keep me sane. I'm so proud of your success, and I can't wait to see what's next for you!

My hubby and girls mean the world to me. Seriously. I cannot adequately express how blessed I feel to call them mine, and it would take an entire book to explain the many ways they supported me while I wrote this book. I *heart* you guys forever and ever.

My mother's always been proud of me, whether warranted or not, but I confess to being nervous about her reaction to the first book in this series. I needn't have worried. After she read it, she told me, "I'm so proud of you—and this book is *hot*." (Insert mortified daughter gif here.) Anyway, I hope you enjoy this one, too, Màe. And thank you for, well, everything.

The rest of my family cheered me on, shared my news, and purchased my book. So in return, I promise to host all of the family's major get-togethers for the next decade. Well, actually, let's start with the ones in 2016 and see how it goes.

Finally, a word about the others members of my "village." I'm sure it's no surprise to anyone that I spend the bulk of my daytime hours either sitting or standing in front of a computer. Most of that time I'm writing. Too much of that time I'm surfing the Internet or trying to figure out the rules for running a Facebook ad. More times than I care to admit, I'm doubting myself and questioning whether my story makes sense or whether I have the "chops" to be a writer. Luckily for me, I have so many people in my life who know just what to say or do to kick those doubts to the curb. And I'm so thankful that my village now includes a host of writers and readers who have generously shared their time, wisdom, and experience with me (I'm looking at you, Soni Wolf, Kerri Carpenter, Sofia Tate, and Ana Coqui). My village is comprised of far too many people to list here, but I have to give a special shout-out to the Dragonflies, the Cackle Corner, my law school tribe, the Binders, and Team Sarah. Sending tackle-hugs to everyone!

CHAPTER ONE

The skin on the back of Karen Ramirez's neck prickled, warning her of the ambush a second before it happened.

Before she could do anything about it, her older sister, Gracie, suddenly appeared in front of Karen and thrust a tumbler in her hand. "Swallow it."

Her sister's best friend, Mimi, erupted into a high-pitched cackle. "That's what he said." The petite blonde donned a coquettish smile and swayed to the music blasting through the club's speakers.

Buoyed by the steady beat of the unfamiliar pop song vibrating around her, Karen gripped the heavy base of the whiskey glass and lifted the drink to her lips. After spending the last four years chained to the desk in her dorm room, she had no clue what to make of the song or the strobe lights flashing through the upscale club in D.C.'s Georgetown neighborhood. It all seemed…a bit much.

She pursed her mouth in distaste at the offending liquid and stared at Gracie with pleading eyes. When that didn't work, she shook her head in tepid refusal.

"It's whiskey, not mouthwash," Mimi pointed out. "Stop swishing it around in your mouth like that."

Okay, might as well get this over with. Karen gulped a generous amount of the honey-colored liquid and thumped a fist over her heart as the burn sped down her chest and settled in her stomach. Disgusting. People drank that crap on purpose?

Gracie, radiant as usual in a sleek black dress, patted Karen's back and smiled. "C'mon, Karen. Relax. It's not every day a Ramirez graduates from college. The books will be there in the morning." Gracie swept her arms in the direction of the dance floor. "For tonight, you need to let loose. Throw caution to the wind."

"Release your inner hussy and screw a hot man," Mimi added as she handed Karen more whiskey, this time in a shot glass.

Gracie's smile faded, and she pinned Mimi with a warning stare. "Whoa there, partner. Rein it in. This is my baby sis you're talking to."

Mimi refused to shrink away. "Your *baby sis* is an adult. And she's entitled to sex, too, Ms. Getting-It-Every-Day-and-Making-the-Rest-of-Us-Jealous."

Gracie covered her ears. "La, la, la. Next subject, please."

Karen waved a hand in front of the dynamic duo. "Hello? I'm here, you know. And while I might be out of practice, I do know how to have fun." She tipped back her head and took another shot. Good lord. Would she grow hair on her chest tonight, too? .

Gracie dropped her hands and gave her sister a sheepish grin. "Sorry, Kar. Anyway, let's find a spot on the dance floor. I want to dance before Ethan gets here."

Karen didn't know her sister's boyfriend well; she'd been so busy at school, most of what she knew about him came from her parents and Gracie. From all reports, he was a good guy, but if he had any possessive tendencies, she and Gracie would have a talk—and then she'd be calling her male cousins in New York to have a "talk" with him.

Karen drew her sister to her side. "Why the rush? He doesn't like you to dance?"

Gracie scoffed. "No, nothing like that. The man has two left feet. I'm saving myself from the embarrassment."

Relieved, Karen took a last shot of whiskey—it went down easier the third time around—and let Gracie lead her to the dance floor, where Mimi had already managed to draw a semicircle of men around her.

Karen's heart rate quickened as strangers' bodies pressed against her. Since she was someone who relished her personal space, this setting made her stomach queasy. Still, Gracie and Mimi were right. It wouldn't hurt to celebrate a little before she buckled down for the road ahead. Four years of medical school. Four years during which she'd have no time for distractions. None. *Rien. Nada.* Tonight, though, she could afford to throw caution to the wind. How much trouble could she get into with her sister in tow anyway?

* * *

Karen groped the wall and tried not to trip as she made her way to the ladies' room. Did the hall have to be so freakin' dark? She pressed her face against the velvet-covered wall, sighing when the soft fabric touched her cheek. Mmmm. Nice.

Speaking of which, whiskey was nice. She'd unfairly maligned the drink before experiencing the heady warmth that spiraled in her belly and radiated out to her limbs. Unfortunately, though, the whiskey also affected her in other, less welcome ways. Every step took more effort than she had energy for, as if she were swimming in a giant vat of chewing gum. And a sheen of perspiration coated her arms. Still, she'd convinced Gracie that she was sober enough to get to the restroom, and she was determined to get there. Otherwise, she'd pee on herself in this swank club.

A few minutes later, after pressing a cool, wet paper towel to her forehead and reapplying her lipstick, Karen left the ladies' room and slammed into a wall. Of chest. She sniffed the dress shirt that covered that chest and grinned. A woodsy scent with a hint of citrus filled her nostrils. Everything was so damn *nice* in this club.

She might have hummed her approval. *Maybe.* And the ensuing silence forced her to realize what she was doing. "You're going to be a gentleman and pretend I didn't sniff you, right?"

Strong hands helped her to remain upright. "Sure. You okay down there?"

The man with the baritone voice didn't bother to hide his amusement at her predicament. She lifted her head, wanting desperately to meet the owner of that voice. And sure enough, the owner did not disappoint. What she could see of him, at least.

Dark hair. Dark eyes. Devilish smile. That smile triggered her sense of self-preservation. *My owner is the mother of all distractions*, it seemed to say. But she held her ground, because if she didn't, she'd topple over in the stilettos Gracie had persuaded her to wear.

She drew back a bit to survey him and experienced an inexplicable urge to snuggle into his massive chest. The shadows across his face highlighted certain features and hinted at others: strong jaw, angular cheekbones, and hair that flopped carelessly over one eyebrow.

He'd asked her a question, but she struggled to remember it. Something about whether she was okay, maybe? Regaining her senses, she stepped out of his loose grasp. "Sorry about that. I'm fine. A celebration gone amuck. The uninitiated should never drink whiskey for the first time in a public place."

"Congratulations on whatever you're celebrating. It looks good on you. You're glowing."

Karen's cheeks warmed. She hoped she wasn't blushing. That would be embarrassing. Hell. Who was she kidding? This encounter had passed *embarrassing* and landed directly on *awkwardly humiliating* when she'd sniffed his shirt. Nevertheless, she managed to thank him, though her voice barely rose above a murmur.

He simply watched her, a ghost of a smile drawing her into his orbit. Of its own volition, her body drifted closer to him.

His eyes, attentive to her every move, narrowed as she came closer. "Are you here alone?"

She must have frowned at the question, because he tripped over himself to explain.

"I'm not trying to pick you up," he said as he raised both hands in the air. "I promise. I don't generally hang out in clubs to pick up women."

Karen focused on the one word that held her interest. "Generally?"

His head rose just a fraction, as though he himself were surprised by his use of the word. "No, not generally. Anyway, I was asking because your…celebration might have affected your faculties, and I'd be an asshat if I didn't make sure you were safe before I left you."

She didn't bother to disagree with his assessment of her faculties, though in truth, the whiskey hadn't completely decimated her senses. "That's sweet." She should have stopped there. But she didn't. "It's also disappointing. I had high hopes for you."

Had she said that out loud? Yes. She. Had. Karen laughed to cover her embarrassment, a weak sound that drifted in the air like a deflated balloon. The buzz from the whiskey had propelled her to act in ways that were foreign to her, erasing the lines she typically didn't cross. Needing to move, she pressed her hand against the back of her neck and winced when a trickle of sweat made its way down her spine. *So attractive.* Whatever. Karen wanted to be daring for a change, sweaty or not. "That didn't come out right. What I meant is, it's a shame that you won't be making a move on me. I'd like you to."

There. She'd said it.

A gaggle of women chose that moment to stumble through the hall on their way to the restroom. He backed up, and when the women had passed, he directed his measured gaze from the top of her head to the toes that peeked out of her abominably painful shoes.

Now that they were separated by a few feet, she surveyed him in his entirety. The business suit hugged his frame as though it had been tailored for him. And judging from its seemingly expensive fabric, it likely had been. Everything about his appearance screamed serious, broody businessman, from the silk tie he hadn't bothered to loosen despite his relaxed surroundings, to the crease between his brows. That is, until you considered his hair, which appeared to follow the whim of his fingers, and the hint of a smile that begged for someone to draw it out completely.

That smile widened when she began to smooth her hands over the front of her dress.

He studied her face. "Nervous, are we?"

"Out of sorts is all."

"A club isn't the best place for a woman to be out of sorts. Be careful. Please."

She didn't detect any censure in his tone, but his words reminded her she knew nothing about this man, and although she wasn't drunk, she wasn't one hundred percent lucid, either. "Thanks for the advice. You're absolutely right."

His eyes went round when he realized she planned to leave, and he reached for her hand. "No. Wait. Stay a minute."

She ignored his hand and moved toward the main area of the club. "I should head back," she said over her shoulder. "This isn't me at all."

"I can tell."

Karen stopped moving and turned to face him. "That obvious, huh?"

"It wasn't meant as an insult, if that's what you're thinking. Just an observation."

"I'm not a specimen in a petri dish, thank you."

He lifted his brows in surprise, and his lips twitched. His face fascinated her. Right now, it said, *I'm intrigued, but I'm not sure if I should engage.* If she were the kind of woman who played strip poker, she would be wise to take advantage of that fact. Without any prompting from her, his face would reveal the strength of his hand, and she'd have him naked in minutes. Karen fanned herself at the thought, and his eyes darted to her jiggling breasts.

He shook his head, as though he needed to clear it, and then his gaze swept across her face. "No, you're not a specimen in a petri dish. Far from it."

Thank goodness he hadn't focused on her breasts. Such blatant ogling would have garnered him a scowl and a first-class ticket to Jerklandia. Plus, she worried her nipples would poke his eyes out. And why was she itchy all of a sudden? *For goodness' sake, Karen, focus.*

He held up his hands. "May I approach?"

She appreciated the question. Would have fled had he moved toward her without gauging her interest. But what was she doing? What did she expect to happen here if he came closer? And when would her sister come looking for her? Karen had been gone more than five minutes, and Gracie had promised to watch for her return. What good was a designated driver without a passenger?

Unsure of his intentions, she nevertheless nodded. But as he walked toward her, her protective instincts kicked in and she changed her mind. "Stop," she said as she raised her hand like a crossing guard.

He stopped mid-stride. "I just want to talk."

"Okay. Let's start with your name."

"Mark."

"Nice to meet you, Mark. I'm Karen. What do you want to talk about?"

"Do you want my gentlemanly response, or the truth?"

She gave him a half smile. "There's a difference?"

He drew his lower lip between his teeth, and Karen nearly melted as she waited for his answer.

"There is," he said after a long pause.

"Let's hear the gentlemanly response first."

"Okay. I'd like to talk to you about your views on the next presidential election."

"Not bad. Now hit me with the truth. What do you really want to talk about?"

"The things I'd do to you if I were free to. I find the idea of talking about them just as enticing as actually doing them."

She raised a single eyebrow and gave him a dubious look. "Really?"

He grinned. "No, not really. But under the circumstances, talking will have to do."

Spurred by his words alone, Karen's brain supplied a barrage of images of them "talking" through the night.

He moved closer, until his breath skated over her ear. "You like that idea, don't you?"

On shaky legs, she tried to suppress her laughter. Dammit. She had to be the most ticklish person ever. If it weren't for that ridiculous fact, the movement of his lips near her ear would have been hot. Instead, though, she struggled not to fall to the ground in a fit of giggles. "Yes, I...I like that idea a lot."

Activating his panty-dropping smile, he reached for her hand. "Come with me?"

Um. Did he really mean that? "Too soon, stranger. We just met."

This time, he rewarded her with a full-blown grin. "I meant follow me."

So she did what any smart woman with too much whiskey in her system would do. She nodded her assent. And then she followed him. Down the hall. Past the emergency exit. Into an alcove with two chairs and a cocktail table nestled between them.

He pointed to one of the chairs, his long, tan fingers catching her attention. "Join me?"

Karen checked the chair bottom for suspicious substances. Finding none, she dropped into it, and the immediate relief to her feet reached orgasmic levels.

Mark waited until she was seated before he took the chair across from her. "Are your feet hurting?"

Ack. That moan hadn't just been in her head? "That's an understatement."

He shifted closer to the edge of his seat, nudged the cocktail table out of the way, and held out his hands. "Let me see."

She wanted to agree to his request, but first she had to address her litany of concerns. She couldn't remember the last time she'd treated herself to a pedicure, and her feet had seen better days. *Much better days.* She was sure they were clean. But she'd been sweating. And what about her heels? She'd been known to do a wicked impression of a woman who kicked flour all day.

He chuckled. "Where did you go?"

"Go?"

"In your head. It's like I lost you for a minute."

Karen tilted her head and sighed. "You did. It's what I do. You could be the most fascinating person in the world, but I tend not to focus on any one thing for long. I have a lot on my mind these days. It's hard for me to turn off my brain and relax."

"Must do wonders for a man's ego."

He didn't mean any harm. To do that, he would have to know about her past relationships with men—which of course, he didn't. Still, the remark stung, and even though she owed him nothing, she regretted the loss of concentration. She dropped her chin. "Sorry about that."

He reached over and lifted her chin. "Nothing to be sorry for.

And if my comment hurt you, I'm the one who should apologize."

This was all getting a little too…deep. Fun. She was supposed to be loosening up and having fun. "It's okay. I'm fine." To prove the truth of that statement, she edged closer to him and lifted her legs. "May I?"

"Yes, set them on my lap."

As she did so, he unbuttoned his suit jacket. She couldn't resist asking him about his choice of clothing. "Do you always wear business suits when you scope out clubs in search of women?"

He flashed his killer grin. "First, as I said before, I don't go to clubs to pick up women."

"Generally."

With a quirk of his lips, he nodded and slipped off her shoes. "Yes, generally. And second, the answer to your question is no. I was dragged here by a friend, and before that I was at a business meeting."

He slid her bare feet along his lap, causing her ankles to press against his muscled thighs. That would have been enough to short-circuit her brain, but he had more in store for her. He ran his fingers down her lower legs and cupped her calves, squeezing them lightly before trailing his fingers down her shins. With the pads of his thumbs pressed against her ankles, he coaxed her legs apart. Just a fraction. Her gaze whipped to his, and he moved his hands away as though her legs had scalded him.

"Too much?" he asked.

Maybe she should have wanted him to stop, but she didn't. "Please. Keep going."

So he resumed his exploration, circling the tops of her feet with the tips of his fingers, their warmth relaxing her and making her go limp. The man possessed magic hands. Smooth. Strong. He kneaded her soles with them, attending to her feet with a deliberateness that led her to envision his hands in more intimate places.

"Tell me what you like," he said.

Karen forced herself not to stutter. "Like?"

He continued to massage her toes. "Sexually."

She opened her mouth to answer him, but her brain had abandoned her.

"Relax. We're just talking. Titillating discussion without having to do the walk of shame in the morning. You liked that idea, remember?"

Yes, she liked the idea, but what could she say? Hell if she knew what she liked. No one had ever bothered to worry about her pleasure, and she'd been too chicken shit to tell them what turned her on. "Honestly? I'm not sure."

His face blanched, and his hands stopped moving. "You've had sex before, right?"

Pfft. Of course she had. But the experiences hadn't been enough to shut off her brain and stop her from blurting out ill-conceived observations. "Yes, I have."

"Tell me. I know there's something you want to say."

"How can you tell?"

"You dip your head to one side and rest your chin on your shoulder, like you want to bury your head in your own neck. You did it before."

Would it be so bad to share her tics with a complete stranger? One she'd never see again? She didn't see any harm in it. "Well, the thing is, I tend to lose my concentration during sex, too." She shook her head, knowing she wasn't explaining herself well. "No. It's more like I tend to think about the wrong things. Or a million things other than sex."

He ran his fingers down her shins and squeezed her ankles. "Give me an example."

Karen shifted her torso away from him and covered her face with her hands. "It's too embarrassing." She peeked through her fingers. "Wait. Are you a therapist or something?"

He lifted a dark brow and shook his head no. "Hardly. We're just talking. And then you'll go off to your life, and I'll go off to mine."

Right. Exactly. "Okay, here's an example. The guy says, 'You're so wet,' because, you know, they *all* say that, and then my brain takes over. And I ask myself, 'Am I? Am I really? Or are you too small? Because I have to say, you're starting to feel like a tampon.'"

He laughed. A deep, rich laugh that made her want to lean over and surprise him with a kiss. He wasn't broody at all. A man who laughed like that, his neck stretched to reveal his Adam's apple and his eyes gleaming in appreciation, could never be broody. Thoughtful? Yes. Broody? No.

"Oh, and I'll never forget the first time a guy went down on me. He lapped at me like a poodle drinking from a water bowl, and I felt nothing."

Mark's shoulders shook after she shared that tidbit.

"I ended up trying to memorize physics formulas until he was done. But that's not all," she continued. "Sometimes I forget that I'm not supposed to articulate my thoughts, or I zone out, and before I know what's happening, the guy, who is rightfully pissed or hurt, scrambles for the door." She removed her feet from his grasp and set them on the floor. Staring at her toes helped her avoid his gaze. "I feel awful. No one should feel inadequate like that, but I can't seem to help myself. And I'm starting to wonder if it's me. You know what I'd love? I'd love to be able to lose myself in the moment, but it's never happened." She shrugged her shoulders. "Someday maybe."

She didn't know what reaction she'd get. Sympathy? Ridicule? Whatever she got, it wouldn't matter. This was about her, not him, because that was the point of catharsis, after all. But when she dared to peek at his face, she nearly fell back against the chair. Lust. There it was. It seeped out of his pores. Darkened his brown eyes to black. Made his big body move with each breath he took. Caused his jaw to go slack.

"Mark?"

When he finally spoke, his voice carried a touch of gravel, a rough sound that she figured only hinted at what he really wanted to say. "What you said just then. Wanting passion that would make you lose all thought and admitting you've never experienced it? That's like waving a flag at a bull. God, there's not much I wouldn't do to get you under me if that's what you wanted. To get you to the point where all you could think about was me. Us. How we fit together. How we moved together."

His words worked their way into her body, filling empty spaces she didn't know she had. What he'd just described? She wanted that, too. She hadn't realized how much until his words had mirrored her thoughts. She burned with the need, in fact. And she squirmed in a feeble attempt to disguise the heat that suffused her. But this was crazy. They'd just met. Her gaze darted around the alcove, the flashy surroundings reminding her that the feelings he'd provoked in her weren't real. It *had* to be the whiskey. The craziness of the night.

Shit. Gracie. Her sister was probably searching for her now. She stood up and held on to the chair as she slipped her shoes back on. "I've got to rejoin my group."

He remained seated, a telltale bulge in his crotch suggesting that standing would be uncomfortable for him. "I'd ask for your last name, but I'm afraid if I knew it, I'd try to find you. And that's not what this is about." He paused. "Right?"

What she'd told him was mortifying, and despite her attraction to him, the knowledge that she'd never see him again would ensure she'd survive the embarrassment. She didn't think long about her answer. "Right. Thanks for the talk, and have a great life, Mark."

Her objective was simple: to infuse her stride with a dab of sexiness and a pinch of confidence. She planned to turn around and leave him with a decent memory of her, one in which she wasn't wobbling away on three-inch stilettos. But her sister's worried voice calling out her name rooted her to the spot.

Seconds later, Gracie skidded into her. "Jesus, Karen. You scared the shit out of me. I've been looking everywhere for you."

Still facing Mark, Karen twisted her head in her sister's direction. "You found me. I'm fine."

Gracie's eyes lit up when she realized that Karen wasn't alone.

For the second time that night, a frisson of dread ran through her. Was that a hint of recognition in Gracie's eyes? No. Fucking. Way. She'd just had one of the most embarrassing conversations ever with a man she'd assumed would remain a stranger. Her sister's face, however, suggested that wouldn't be the case. Karen quite literally prayed she'd read Gracie wrong.

But crap on a crostini, Gracie's frown suddenly changed to a broad grin. "Mark? Is that you?"

CHAPTER TWO

Mark watched the train wreck in front of him. The woman who'd crashed into his life, that is. He wanted to look away, but his brain refused to cooperate. Drawn to Karen by something he couldn't explain, he cataloged her every move. So he'd known the minute she'd decided to walk away from him forever, to place him squarely in her mental Rolodex as the man who'd fondled her footsies that night long ago when she'd had one whiskey too many. And he'd just witnessed the barely suppressed horror on her face when she'd realized her sister knew him.

This was Gracie's baby sister? Gracie was his best friend's girlfriend. And given how happy Ethan seemed to be lately, owing in large part to Gracie, Mark figured he'd have to interact with Karen at some point. Christ. The things she'd told him. The things he'd said in response. He couldn't undo any of it. And judging from Karen's wooden demeanor, she'd come to the same conclusion.

Maybe he could salvage the situation, though, with some acting on his part. Maybe, just maybe, he'd inherited his mother's flair for drama and would be able to play off their encounter in a way that wouldn't embarrass Karen.

He stood, buttoned his suit jacket, and offered Gracie his hand. "Gracie. Good to see you."

Gracie sidestepped his outstretched hand and hugged him. "Stop acting ridiculous, Mark. Ethan's been looking for you. We wanted to get everyone together."

When Gracie released him, he stumbled back—that's what people did when they were drunk, right? "Sheesh. I guess I had too much Scotch tonight." He donned a dazed expression, hoping to make his performance convincing. Given that he'd just said "Sheesh," he doubted his success.

Oblivious to the tension, Gracie turned to her sister and drew her forward, forming a circle with their bodies. The circle of hell couldn't have been any worse than this. "You guys saved me a step. I see you already met my baby sister."

Karen grimaced. "Younger sister."

Gracie flinched at Karen's sharp tone, but her face remained calm. "Right. *Younger sister.* Karen just graduated from college, and we're celebrating that amazing accomplishment. Starts medical school at George Washington in the fall." Gracie beamed with pride. "She'll be the first doctor in our family." She covered her mouth and leaned toward him. "Not that we're pressuring her or anything."

Mark wished he were a beaver so he could tunnel through the floor, leaving a cloud of dust in his wake as he escaped. If Karen had just graduated from college, that made her...what? Twenty-one? Twenty-two, at most? Which meant he was almost eleven years her senior. He'd called himself plenty of unflattering names over the years, but now he could add "cradle robber" to that illustrious list.

And he cursed his father's genes, the ones that had led him to be attracted to someone who was all wrong for him.

His resolve to erase whatever had happened between them moments ago solidified. "Yes. She mentioned a celebration. Dara, was it?" He hit his forehead with the heel of his hand. "Sorry. Kara, right?"

Karen squished her eyebrows together and frowned. "It's Karen."

He wished he could tell her he'd never forget her name. Wished he could tell her he wanted to take her home, have sex with her against a shower wall, and end round two in his king-size bed. But that wasn't going to happen. One, she was Gracie's sister. Two, she was Gracie's *baby* sister. And three, relationships weren't his forte—*his problem, of course, not hers*—and the alternative, a no-strings hookup, was out of the question, because of…points one and two.

He loosened his tie, and then he ran his fingers through his hair. "Forgive me, Karen. It's been a long, frustrating day, and the liquor hasn't helped set my head straight. Next time we talk, I'll promise to remember your name and what we talked about."

Her head snapped back, and she formed an O with that lovely mouth of hers. In his head, he urged her to go with it, to suspend disbelief just enough to save them from further embarrassment. For several taut seconds, it appeared she wouldn't make it easy for either of them. But then she donned a placid expression, a tremulous smile undermining the ease she no doubt sought to convey. "No worries, Mark. I'm sure it was gibberish anyway."

Karen looped her arm through Gracie's and smiled. "You said you wanted to get us together?"

Gracie, who'd pulled out her phone and was texting someone,

raised her head and grinned. "Yes. Let's head back to the table. Ethan's there. We have a surprise for you guys."

As Gracie and Karen walked ahead of him, he fought the urge to stare at Karen's ass. A surprise? Shit. He could do without any more surprises today.

When they reached the counter-height cocktail table, Ethan took Gracie's hand and led her to stand beside him. His best friend looked more relaxed than Mark had ever seen him. And when Ethan raised Gracie's hand to his lips and gave it a quick kiss, Mark suspected an engagement announcement would follow. That bothered him more than he cared to admit. There it was. The truth. He wouldn't begrudge Ethan the happiness he deserved, but the fact that Ethan had found that happiness, through a committed relationship and in the arms of an incredible woman, heightened Mark's awareness that he'd never sought the same for himself.

Mark chose relationships with short expiration dates instead. It was easier that way. He had a multimillion-dollar communications company to worry about, he reasoned. He couldn't give any woman the time or attention it would take to cultivate a serious relationship. And the last thing he'd ever want to do was make a woman feel expendable, unimportant, as though she didn't matter in his world; not letting a woman into his world ensured he'd never do that.

But that didn't mean he couldn't show a woman a good time. Treat her like a queen. Make her happy in some small way. He'd been lucky enough to meet women looking for precisely what he offered. Great sex. Fun times. No commitment. And when work called him away, as it invariably did, his companion would give him a soft peck on the cheek and nod in understanding. His lifestyle suited him.

Looking at Gracie and Ethan now, however, Mark acknowledged the twinge in his chest might just be envy.

Gracie shifted behind Ethan, her nervous smile all but confirming Mark's initial suspicion. She wrapped her arms around Ethan's waist and rested her chin on his shoulder. "We're getting married. In three weeks."

Boom. The announcement settled in his gut like an anchor, heavy and unyielding.

Mimi's eyes nearly popped out of her head. "Holy shit, Gracie. What happened? You didn't wrap any casing around that sausage and got knocked up?"

Gracie dropped her forehead onto Ethan's shoulder. "*Sinvergüenza*. No, I'm not pregnant."

Mark leaned into Karen. "What's *sinvergüenza*?"

Eyes wide, Karen whispered her response. "A shameless person. Look up *sinvergüenza* in a Spanish dictionary and a photograph of someone who bears a startling resemblance to Mimi will be there."

She'd moved closer to him, a fact he couldn't ignore. Her sweet scent wafted around him, and he had to stop himself from reaching for her, from tucking her into him and proclaiming his interest in her. But that would have been impossible in any event, because she bolted across the small space, shoved Ethan out of the way, and enveloped Gracie in a fierce hug. "Congratulations, Gracie. You're happy, right? That's all that matters." She lowered her voice, which nevertheless carried across the group. "But why the rush?"

Ethan slapped Mark on the back. "It's his fault."

With all eyes directed at him, Mark tried to appear unruffled by the declaration. "My fault? How so?"

"You're the one who moved up the timing of the KisNet launch.

If we're going to get that software ready to go before the holiday season, I won't be able to take off any time in the fall."

Gracie squeezed Karen's hand. "We don't want a big wedding, just a few friends and family. And I'd like our grandmother to be there, so the important thing is to make it happen while we can."

Karen furrowed her brows. "Abuela Marta?"

Gracie nodded. "Yes."

"But she's never going to leave the island."

Gracie nodded again. "I know. So we plan to take the wedding to her."

Mimi waved her hands in the air like she was partying on the dance floor. "Puerto Rico? I am *so* there. I could use a few days in the sun."

A wedding in three weeks. On the island of Puerto Rico. Mark gave the couple credit for focusing on what they wanted as opposed to what others might expect of them. "Well, congratulations to you both. I'm really happy for you. It sounds like fun. And Ethan, take all the time you need. The KisNet launch will be here when you get back."

Ethan laid a hand on his shoulder. "Not so fast, buddy. I need a best man, and you can't say no. You're coming with us."

Mark's stomach flipped. "To Puerto Rico?"

Ethan smiled. "Yeah. Mimi, too. And Karen, of course."

Mark darted a glance at Karen's expressive face, which this minute had a delightful flush to it.

Right. And Karen, of course. Because that's just what his overactive imagination and underserved libido needed. Miles and miles of beautiful beach, sun-kissed skies, sweltering, sticky nights, and Karen.

He couldn't think with everyone staring at him, waiting for his answer, so he said enough to pacify Ethan. "If I can adjust my schedule to make it work, I will. But I can't make any promises."

Ethan nodded. "Sure, sure. Just let me know soon."

Whatever lie he could tell to get out of this jaunt, he needed to come up with it fast.

CHAPTER THREE

The man lied as well as she drank.

Karen knew he hadn't been drinking when they met. After all, he'd been the one to claim he couldn't pursue her precisely because she'd been tipsy. She knew that. He knew that. Hell, she knew he knew *she* knew that.

As she watched Mark hand the valet a tip and slide into his Aston Martin, a sleek, silver number that attracted the envious attention of passersby, Karen considered their initial meeting. When Mimi's car arrived, he revved his engine. Before he pulled away, he tipped his head in her direction and tapped on the red fur dice dangling from the rearview mirror. That about summed up her take on Mark: He was a walking curveball. And that was the reason she hadn't stopped thinking about his lie. She hadn't known what to make of it.

But now that the effects of the whiskey had faded, she came to the embarrassing conclusion that she'd made such an ass of herself he'd had no other choice but to make the episode disappear in a puff of smoke. *Abracadabra.* Gone. Never to be spoken of again.

That was fine with her. Actually kind of sweet on his part. And for the best, too. She'd always rejected the idea of a committed relationship, precisely because she had neither the inclination nor the time to date anyone. Her past foibles in the bedroom had rid her of the desire for a lover. Why put herself through the awkwardness of another unsuccessful attempt at sex? Plus, when she started medical school in the fall, she'd be on permanent lockdown anyway. No dating. No social life. No nothing.

So thinking about Mark *in that way* was pointless. Yes, pointless.

Except the memory of his reaction when she'd told him about her inability to relax during sex called to her like nothing ever had before. In that moment, her embarrassment over her past failures in the bedroom had receded, replaced by the promise of becoming the lover she'd always wanted to be. Confident. Sensual. *Attentive.* Her instincts told her Mark would help her become that person or die trying.

Mimi waved a hand in front of Karen's face. "Hello? You okay?"

She shook her head, more so to give herself time to respond than to clear her brain. She didn't want her expression to reveal her thoughts about Mark. "I'm fine. The whiskey's definitely gone to my head. Thanks for the ride home. Gracie and Ethan clearly needed some alone time."

Mimi grimaced as she fished in her purse. "Dammit. Finding money in this purse is like searching for a dick in a bushel of corn on the cob." She pulled out a few bills for the valet. "No need to thank me for the ride. Gracie's family is my family."

She'd never admit it, but Karen envied Gracie and Mimi's relationship. Always had. Their relationship sprang from friendship rather than obligation. And while some might consider Mimi high-maintenance, Karen knew Mimi had her sister's back. Always. High-maintenance or not, friends like her were not easy to find. "Well, I appreciate it anyway."

Mimi ducked into the car, and Karen buckled herself into the passenger seat.

A thought occurred to her then. What if Mimi was interested in Mark? It would be great if she was, actually. That way, Karen would have no choice but to step aside and stuff any thoughts about Mark into the forbidden closet. Wait. Mark. In a closet. With her. Doing forbidden stuff. *No, no, no.*

She took out a compact and pretended to check her lipstick. "So what do think of Mark?"

Hands on the steering wheel, Mimi whipped her head in Karen's direction and narrowed her eyes before returning her attention to the road ahead. "I don't. Why do you ask?"

"Oh, I just wondered if he was a prospect for you. You two would be cute together."

Goodness, she was just as bad a liar as Mark was.

Mimi arched a brow and shook her head from side to side. "Mark is definitely not a prospect."

"You wouldn't pursue him?"

"Nope."

"Huh."

"Now, don't get me wrong. I'd bang that in a hot minute. But he's Ethan's best friend, and Ethan's practically my brother-in-law. I suspect I'm a little too headstrong for him. And I like a bit of Tarzan in my men. Mark doesn't give off that vibe. So the odds of any relationship between us working out hovers around zero to zero. Plus..."

"Plus what?"

"Plus I don't roam in my own backyard."

"What the hell does that mean?"

"It means when I send a guy packing, I want him gone. I can't guarantee that with Mark."

Karen kicked off her stilettos. "You have a point."

Unfortunately, Mimi hadn't erected the barrier Karen was hoping for. And worse, the reasons Mimi discounted Mark as a prospect were the very reasons why he tempted Karen. No long-term relationship would arise from any tryst between them. And he resided in her own backyard, a convenient fact given that she didn't want or have time to get to know someone outside her small social circle. But she had no business contemplating a liaison with Mark, she reminded herself, not with medical school barreling toward her. She'd worked hard to get to this point, and no man would deter her from focusing on her career.

At the end of the summer, she'd disappear into the world of a sleep-deprived medical student, never to be heard from again. Until then—and probably well beyond then, too—she'd work out her desires with the help of her battery-powered life partner. So what if Mark would feature prominently in her fantasies? That would be a secret between her and her vibrator.

CHAPTER FOUR

I think it's time for me to settle down."

Mark and Ethan ran along the C&O Canal Trail in Washington, D.C., their favorite place to exercise on Sunday mornings. He needed the stress relief, especially after a restless night in which he'd been unable to do anything but think about Karen.

To Mark's left, an old lock house sat near a narrow expanse of the canal, hidden from the sun by the overgrown foliage surrounding it. He breathed in the smell of wet grass, a remnant of the morning's sun shower. Peace. It hung in the air and comforted him. Engrossed by his surroundings, it took him several steps to realize Ethan no longer ran beside him.

When he turned, his friend was doubled over, hands on his knees. Mark spun around and jogged backward. "You okay, Ethan?"

Ethan sucked in air and squinted at him. "I'm fine. The real question is, are you okay? Did I just hear you correctly?" Ethan straightened and walked toward him. "If I did, the apocalypse must be upon us."

Mark took that as a sign they wouldn't be running the rest of the trail, so he whipped off his T-shirt and swiped it across his sweaty chest. "I'll be honest, your engagement to Gracie has something to do with it. It got me thinking about my own future. Maybe it's time to stop messing around and find a wife."

Ethan picked up a rock, threw it into the canal, and walked beside him. "Interesting."

Mark watched the rock skip across the water and disappear. He expected honesty from Ethan. Always. But the pensive look on Ethan's face suggested his friend was holding something back. "Go ahead and say what you're thinking, E."

Ethan sighed. "Let me preface this by saying, I'm not judging you, just noticing things. You're a bachelor. Rich. Relatively good-looking. You're obviously discreet, too, because you don't talk about your sex life all that often. And the next thing I know, you're talking about finding a wife. Not a girlfriend. Not someone to fall in love with. A wife. As though you have to check some box that fits into your life plan."

Damn. When Ethan described it that way, Mark saw his point. And maybe he *was* going about this all wrong. But last night's festivities, from his run-in with Karen to Ethan and Gracie's engagement, had spurred him to want to work on his own love life, and he couldn't shake the sense that he needed to be quick about it. Otherwise, he'd end up like his father. Alone. Still pining for someone he should have stayed away from. The trouble was, he'd been dodging a serious relationship for so long he didn't know where to begin.

If he tried to cultivate a relationship on his own, he'd resume his old habits and use his busy work schedule as an excuse to avoid spending any meaningful time with a woman. A ride on his boat?

Easy. A weekend trip to Paris? Not a problem. But a sustained effort to talk to a woman and get to know her? Clueless.

Then it had occurred to him. If Ethan and Gracie were involved, they'd force him to make an effort; if nothing else, he'd follow through to avoid pissing them off. Accountability. That's what he needed.

Ethan cleared his throat. "Mark."

"Yeah?"

"You're a planner. I get that. You even schedule your relaxation time down to the minute."

"C'mon, man, you're exaggerating."

Ethan stopped and gave him a wide-eyed stare. "Oh, yeah? What'd you tell me this morning about when you needed to get back?"

Mark thought about it and mumbled his response.

Ethan laughed and cupped his ear. "Excuse me? What was that?"

"I said I had to be back by ten thirty-five."

With a triumphant gleam in his eyes, Ethan slapped him on his shoulder. "Exactly. Not ten thirty. Not even a quarter to eleven. Ten thirty-five. Every minute of your life can't be planned. That's not how it works. And if my experience with Gracie taught me anything, it's that you can't plan love."

"I know that, E. I'm not trying to plan love. I'm simply trying to do things a little differently this time. And I'm man enough to admit I need help. Yours and Gracie's, specifically."

"I'm flattered, man." Ethan waggled his eyebrows. "And you came to the right person, too. I'm a bit of a connoisseur when it comes to matters of the heart."

"I know this, E. In fact, if you weren't committed to Gracie, I'd date you myself." Mark wrapped his arm around Ethan's shoulder. "Plus, you're so fucking hot, I can't stand it."

Ethan rested his head on Mark's shoulder and batted his eyelashes. "Really? Tell me what makes me so hot. I'm not fishing for compliments or anything, but I'd like to know."

Ethan pushed Mark's arm off him and twisted his waist as he bent into an overly dramatic runner's stretch. After several seconds of that ridiculousness, he straightened and flexed his biceps. "It's the guns, right? Gracie loves them."

Mark barked out a laugh. "Nope. It's that big, bulging…brain that makes you so hot. It's so huge, it's a wonder you can keep it under a hat."

"Yeah, I get that a lot. Okay, back to the finding a wife thing. Let's not call it that. Let's not call it anything, for that matter. Let me and Gracie set you up. No pressure. No expectations. If you find a wife, fine. If you find the love of your life, great. The point is, you're looking for something more than casual, right?"

"Right."

"Okay, Gracie will eat this up. So give me the details. What kind of woman are you looking for?"

Mark's thoughts turned to Karen. Gracie would clobber him if he showed any interest in her "baby" sister, particularly because she'd convinced herself he embraced his bachelor status with more enthusiasm than most. On this issue, she and Ethan agreed. They both swore he was hiding a harem. Neither was right, but he'd never disabused either of them of their incorrect assumptions.

He approached his answers to Ethan's questions with two purposes in mind. One, he sincerely wanted to give Ethan information that would be helpful to the task. Two, he needed to remind himself how incompatible he and Karen were, so he could move on with no regrets. "I'd like to meet a woman around my age. A professional in a good rhythm career-wise." In other words, someone nothing like Karen. "Someone busy like me who would understand the pressure of our respective positions and wouldn't make unreasonable demands on my time." Karen probably wouldn't make unreasonable demands on his time, though. Soon, she'd be a medical student. Great. Just like that, he'd circled back to Karen.

Ethan pretended to scribble notes on a pad. "Okay. What else?"

"Settled." As his father had told him countless times before, Mark's mother had nearly suffocated under the burden of being tied down to a husband and a kid well before she was ready. He wouldn't repeat his parents' mistakes. "She should be settled in life."

"Meaning what?"

They'd reached a fork in the trail, a weathered bench marking the spot where bikers were no longer permitted to ride. Ethan sat on the bench, and Mark followed suit. Mark raised his face to the sun, enjoying the warmth of its rays on his skin. "She's figured out the answers to the big questions. What she wants to be when she grows up. Where she wants to live. The kind of man she'd enjoy spending time with."

Ethan nodded. "Got it. What about children?"

Mark imagined a life without kids. Definitely doable, but someone who'd rule out raising children altogether was probably a non-starter. "She should be receptive to the idea of children, let's start with that."

"Throw out some traits."

"Confidence, both socially and in the bedroom. That's a definite turn-on."

"I'm not sure I'd be able to vet someone on their confidence in the bedroom. Gracie would flash-fry my balls in a skillet."

Ouch. "For fuck's sake, Ethan, that's not even funny. Let's focus on confidence in general, then."

"Okay. What about physical traits? I have no idea whether you're a leg man or a breast man."

Mark waggled his eyebrows. "I'm partial to wings, actually."

Ethan simply stared at him and that blank stare prodded Mark to take the question seriously. He winced when a vision of Karen's face popped into his head. Fucking Karen. Her image refused to go away.

She wore her long, dark brown hair loose, a mass of waves dancing around her heart-shaped face. What was the opposite of that? Oh, that was easy. "I'm not one to pick apart a woman's features, but I like the sexy librarian look. Hair pulled back, black-framed glasses."

"Back to the breasts and ass. Which do you prefer, or is it both?"

Mark didn't have to think long about that one. "If I could have both, I'd die a happy man. I'm a leg man, too."

Now Karen's legs, hers he liked a lot. Long, toned, and smooth. The minute he'd touched them, he'd regretted it. The move implied an intimacy neither he nor she had been prepared for. If he saw her again, and he had every expectation he would, he'd know that her calves were strong and that if he applied just the right pressure to the backs of her knees, she'd moan her appreciation.

This. Was not. Helping.

Ethan rubbed his hands together, a lopsided grin transforming his face from pensive to conniving. "That's enough for Gracie and me to work with. You'll have to give us a little latitude, okay? If this is going to work, you're going to have to relinquish some control."

Fat chance there. The thought of losing control made him queasy. And these days more than most, he hated the idea of losing control. He liked plans. Order. Organization. Without them, the slippery slope led to chaos. And given his tumultuous childhood, chaos was not an option. "I won't pretend to like it, but I'll do my best to give you the latitude you need."

Ethan slapped a hand on his shoulder. "Excellent. I have a great feeling about this. As soon as Gracie and I return from Puerto Rico, we'll get on it. Unless you meet someone there, of course."

Ethan had just given him the conversational opening he needed to bail on the trip, but he couldn't muster the assholery to take it. He'd suck it up and go, no matter how uncomfortable things might be between him and Karen. With any luck, and perhaps in tacit agreement, they'd limit their exposure to each other until their initial encounter was no longer fresh in their minds. And when he returned from Puerto Rico, he'd focus on finding a serious girlfriend. A potential wife, even. But for now, he had a wedding to attend—and a woman to avoid.

CHAPTER FIVE

Gracie would kill them if they missed this flight.

Karen paced in front of the departure gate at the airport. As far as she could tell, the other two members of their impromptu wedding party hadn't arrived yet. But Gracie, who'd traveled with Ethan to Puerto Rico a few days ago, had warned her that Mimi rarely got to the airport on time.

The airline personnel busied themselves with pre-flight procedures, and one of them hovered near the microphone, ready to announce the start of boarding. Karen searched the faces in the crowd. Unless Mimi and Mark caught this flight, they'd likely miss the pre-wedding dinner that evening. Karen wanted everything to be perfect for her sister's celebration, so the thought of the bride and groom's closest friends not being there made her anxious. Her rattled nerves had *nothing* to do with the fact that Mark would be joining them on the flight to San Juan. *Nothing.* Besides, Mark would be settled comfortably in the first-class cabin, far away from the screaming babies and manspreading she and Mimi would be forced to endure in coach.

Her agita didn't last long. Within minutes, she spotted Mimi walking toward her and breathed a sigh of relief. Before Karen could say hello, Mimi thrust a T-shirt in her hand. "Here. Put this on. To identify us as members of the wedding party."

Karen smirked. "All three of us, you mean?"

Mimi gave her a pointed stare. "Look, your sister sprung this wedding on us out of nowhere. She's my best friend, and I will *not* be denied my bridesmaid experience. Just work with me, please."

Karen looked at Mimi's shirt and blinked. Then she blinked some more. Mimi's T-shirt identified her as a BRIDESMAID. That was plain enough. But just below that one word, she'd customized the T-shirt to read, ASSIGNMENT: TO BLOCK COCKS.

Dumbfounded, Karen pointed to Mimi's chest. "What in the world, Mimi?"

Unfazed by Karen's question, Mimi popped her glossed lips and leaned in. "I'm keeping the lovebirds apart until their wedding night."

"Why?"

Mimi purred and formed kitten claws with her hands. "After a few days of deprivation, they'll be ravenous for each other. Cue the mind-blowing sex."

"Is this normal, Mimi? The level of concern you have for my sister's sex life, I mean."

"Look, I'm not getting any these days. I'm living vicariously through her. And with several margaritas in her system, Gracie blurts out delicious stories."

"Eww. Gross. I don't want to know this about you. Or my sister."

"Fine. But you're missing out on good stuff."

"I'm happy to sit out on those lovely conversations, thank you."

Remembering the T-shirt in her own hand, Karen whipped it in front of her and expelled a relieved breath when she saw only the word BRIDESMAID across the chest area. At least Mimi had the good sense not to expect Karen to join her crazy train. Plus, she suspected any minute now the airline would ask Mimi to take off the shirt, particularly given the children who were waiting to board.

Sure enough, seconds later, a ticket agent rounded the counter and walked up to Mimi. "Ma'am, may I have a word with you?"

Mimi shuffled off with the attendant as Karen dropped into a nearby seat to watch the theatrics. Less than a minute into his explanation, the attendant backed away as Mimi alternated between pointing at the shirt and gesturing wildly. Karen sank farther into her seat. After a tense standoff, Mimi stood on her toes, reached across the counter for a marker, and wrote directly on her shirt. She pinned the attendant with a stare that challenged him to object to her modification. The poor man's ears turned crimson, and then he reluctantly nodded his approval.

With a triumphant smile on her face, Mimi returned to her seat, a *j* having replaced the *c*—sort of. Karen laughed. Much easier for the parents on the plane to suffer through a million questions about what it meant to *block jocks* than it would have been to sidestep questions about Mimi's original phrasing.

Mimi grumbled as she riffled through her purse. "Morons. Now everyone's going to think I'm a linebacker."

Karen couldn't help laughing again. "I think people are going to know exactly what you meant to say. And to be fair, Mimi, there are kids on this plane. Think of all those impressionable minds you'd sully with your T-shirt."

"Why would those kids stare at my chest anyway?" Mimi pursed her lips, considering her own question. "No, forget I asked that. These boobs are phenomenal. But that's not really the point. The bigger question is, why are children even allowed to fly on planes?"

She knew Mimi didn't expect an answer, and that was just as well, because Karen almost swallowed her tongue when she spotted Mark. *Well, hello there.*

He wore a white linen shirt, unbuttoned at the top so that a hint of his tanned chest peeked out. And he'd rolled up the sleeves, putting his muscled forearms on display. She studied his approach, noting the relaxed pants and slip-on shoes that completed his casual look.

He reminded her of one of the models she'd seen in fashion magazines, except that he didn't appear to be sucking in his cheeks, and he had enough bulk to leave no doubt in her mind that he never missed a meal. The man carried his good looks and impressive stature with ease, nothing forced or disingenuous about him. She glanced down at her own outfit—a baby blue T-shirt and skinny jeans—and marveled at the difference between her travel wear and his. So. Not. Fair.

He strode to the counter, where an all-too eager attendant proceeded to attend to him. The overly solicitous smile on the woman's face suggested she was prepared to fulfill his nonflying needs, too.

Mimi bumped Karen's shoulder with her own. "*Pssst.*"

Karen snapped out of her Mark-induced trance. "What?"

"You dropped something."

Karen bent at the waist and searched the floor around her. "What? Where?"

Mimi pointed her finger at Karen's feet. "Over there. Your jaw."

Karen whipped her head in Mimi's direction and registered Mimi's ear-to-ear smile. "Cute. And you're seeing things."

"Don't get your panties all twisted. It's painful." Mimi waggled her eyebrows. "Or pleasurable depending on the circumstances."

"Mimi."

"Well, all I'm saying is if your underwear is in just the right place, you can tug and twist it and bring yourself to—"

"Mimi."

"What? Oh, right. Look, there's nothing wrong with appreciating a good-looking man."

"Exactly. That's all it is."

Mimi nodded. "Good. Gracie would drive you nuts otherwise. And I get it, okay? I mean, look at him. I'd bang that drum, too. All I'm saying is, if you don't want your overprotective sister meddling in your business, find someone else to massage your lady bits."

"I'm partial to massaging my own lady bits, actually. I have no problem getting my own kinks out."

"Yes, well, more power to you then. But I, for one, am getting carpal tunnel syndrome with all the self-massaging I've been doing as of late."

Karen snickered. She did that often when she was in Mimi's presence. Out of the corner of her eye, she tracked Mark's progress toward them. "Zip it. He's on his way over."

Mimi straightened and held out her hand. "Hey, Mark. Good to see you again."

"Mimi, nice to see you, too."

With her eyes averted and her smile frozen in place, Karen waited for him to acknowledge her, in part because she wanted to see how he would approach their first meeting since the night at the club, but mostly because she didn't know what else to do.

"Hello, Karen."

Oh, my. She'd heard his voice before, but this was different. He'd lowered it to just above a whisper, her name leaving his mouth as softly as a caress. This greeting was personal. Intimate. Like they'd already had sex and he wanted to let her know how much he'd enjoyed it.

Mimi cleared her throat. "So, Mark, while you're up there hobnobbing with the one percenters, could you snag us a couple of high-end cocktails? And a clean blanket?"

He raised an eyebrow, an adorable look of confusion upping his hotness factor by ten. "You're not in first-class?"

Mimi laughed. "No. I'm all out of frequent flyer miles."

Karen shrugged. "Recent college graduate here."

As soon as the words left her mouth, Karen regretted them. But it was the truth. And even if funds hadn't been tight, a first-class ticket was a luxury she'd forgo for a more tangible item. Like a kick-ass pair of boots.

Mark met her gaze, a question in his eyes. "I assumed Ethan and Gracie were paying for you. They didn't offer?"

Karen nodded. "They tried. We refused. They're paying for the hotel rooms. The least we could do was spring for the flight."

He tipped his head and ran his tongue over his top lip. He did it in slow motion. Or at least her mind registered it as such.

Sweet Jesus. Did he really have to sexify every one of his actions?

When she looked up, he flicked his gaze to a spot behind her. Then he reached into his pocket and pulled out his phone. "Excuse me. I forgot I have to make a call."

He refused to meet her gaze and his face suggested he was mentally a million miles away. Dammit. She'd been staring at his lips, and she'd made him uncomfortable.

"Of course," she said.

Karen watched him walk away just as the airline announced the start of boarding. Five minutes in his presence and he'd left her flustered.

Mimi tugged on her arm. "Run to the bathroom and put your shirt on. We still have plenty of time."

Right. She could use a few minutes to regroup.

* * *

Mimi, the rat, had purchased a small T-shirt for her. Tiny, in fact. So tiny she might as well have been wearing pasties. Karen debated whether to take it off, but once the PA system had announced the boarding of their flight, she threw her denim jacket over the T-shirt and scrambled out of the restroom.

She found Mimi hovering near the gate.

"All set?" Mimi asked.

"Yes, but I should bitch-slap you for the size of my T-shirt."

Mimi grinned. "Or you could thank me for being so thoughtful. You look perky."

"*Grrr.*"

Mimi patted Karen's head. "Now, now, my pet. Be nice or I'll neuter you."

Karen swiped Mimi's hand away and leaned against a post to await their turn to board.

Mark walked past them and waved. "Have a nice flight, ladies. See you in San Juan."

Mimi stuck her tongue out at him, and though he'd already walked past them, Karen caught the tail end of his laughter.

She and Mimi trudged through the jet bridge and made it on the plane. Mark sat next to another handsome man, this one in a business suit. They'd probably spend the entire flight discussing stocks and bonds or something. She spied a couple ahead of her arguing over where to store their luggage, so she parked her carry-on by her foot. *Lovely.*

Mimi winked at the pilots as she passed them. "Can I see your cock? Um, *cockpit*. I meant, *Can I see your cockpit?*"

A woman behind them cackled. "Can I see it, too?"

Karen fussed with the collar of her denim jacket, wanting desperately to bury her face in it. She turned just in time to see Mark shake his head at Mimi's remark. A man across the aisle from Mark stared at Karen, a little too closely for her liking, and with nothing to do but wait for the passengers ahead of her to get settled, she dug into her pocket and pulled her hair back into a haphazard ponytail. When she was done, she peeked at the man and found him still watching her. Mark volleyed his gaze between the man and Karen, his knitted brow furrowing and relaxing within seconds.

Finally, she and Mimi settled into their seats, Mimi taking the window seat because, according to her, she'd be less likely to drool on Karen if Mimi fell asleep.

Karen dug in her purse for her e-reader, more than ready to dive into a romance novel about a female mechanic and a buttoned-up businessman. But her quest for a little relaxation was short-lived.

A flight attendant with a plastic smile and a bored expression stopped at their row and cleared her throat. "Ladies, we have two seats available in first-class. Would you like to take those instead?"

Mimi jumped up. "Hell, yes!"

Karen had a less enthusiastic reaction. "Why us?"

"One of our first-class passengers thought you might appreciate an upgrade. If you'd prefer to decline, I can deliver that message." She said this in all seriousness, and punctuated the last word with a lift of her perfectly arched brows. In other words, *If you want to be an idiot and turn down better accommodations, be my guest.*

Mark. He must have arranged for the upgrade.

Mimi sucked her teeth. "Really, Karen. What's to think about?"

Karen leaned over and glanced down the aisle. Someone else deserved the upgrade more than she did. "There's a Marine on this flight," she told the flight attendant. "I saw him on my way in. Can you offer it to him, in appreciation for his service?"

The flight attendant smiled, this time appearing genuine in her friendliness. "Mr. Lansing took care of that passenger, too. He's already in first-class."

Mimi pushed past her, knocking Karen back into her seat. "See? All taken care of. Let's go."

Karen fought the urge to overthink the significance of Mark's offer. Would it be so bad to simply accept the offer for what it was: a friendly gesture by someone with the financial means to do them a favor? She worried her bottom lip in contemplation. Meanwhile, Mimi grabbed her bag from the overhead and sprinted down the empty aisle. "It's been real, folks. See you in San Juan."

As Karen rolled her suitcase down the aisle, she mentally practiced what she would say to Mark about upgrading her seat to first-class.

Thank you, but you didn't have to do that. No, what would be the point of stating the obvious? Of course he didn't have to do it. He'd *chosen* to do it. Probably on a whim.

Thank you, that was really sweet of you. No, that would sound desperate, like she was attaching more significance to the gesture than was warranted. The man had the money to pay for the upgrade, or a bajillion frequent flyer miles to cover it. Surely the upgrade wasn't a big deal to him.

Thank you, I've never sat in first-class before. If she needed a neon sign to highlight her lack of sophistication, telling him she was a first-class cabin virgin would do rather nicely. Uh, definitely a no.

So she settled on *thank you.* And when she drew back the curtain, Mark rose from his seat and reached for her carry-on. His smile could not have been more appealing.

"Let me help you with that," he said.

"Sure, thanks. Listen, about the upgrade, I appreciate it. You didn't have to do it, of course." She crossed her eyes. "I mean, I *know* you didn't have to do it, and that was really sweet of you. But maybe not such a big deal, right? What, with all your frequent flyer miles. Still, that was a nice thing to do. Not that I'm reading anything into it. Yeah, that wouldn't make sense." She gave a weak laugh. "I've never been in first-class before." *Why the hell were her ears burning all of a sudden?* She clapped her hands together like a seal, hoping to snap herself out of her mental runs. "Should be an experience." And as if that stunning soliloquy were not enough, she ended it with a sigh that came out as a horrendous wheezing sound.

Good Lord, she needed a muzzle.

Saving Karen from further embarrassment, the flight attendant tapped Mark on his shoulder. "We'll need you both in your seats, please. The plane will be ready to leave the gate soon."

Karen whipped her head around and searched for her seat. Mimi had already finagled a spot next to the Marine, after asking his original seatmate to switch places.

Because they'd all apparently decided to play musical chairs, Mark's seatmate rose. "Since you guys know each other, I'll move. That way you can sit together."

Karen glanced at Mark in time to see the tic in his jaw. Well, he might not appreciate the opportunity for them to sit next to each other, but she'd take it anyway, because the alternative was to sit next to the creepy dude in 3B. "That would be great," she said to the Suit. "I really appreciate that. He's the best man at my sister's wedding, so we can chat about the toasts and stuff."

Mark nodded. "Right. *And stuff.*"

"Okay if I take the window seat?"

Mark hesitated. "Sure."

"Great."

She took a gingerly step around Mark and scanned her upgraded accommodations. *Very nice.* Big, comfy seats made of buttery gray leather. Tray tables trimmed in wood paneling. And flight attendants who rushed to bring the passengers drinks even before takeoff. Oh, and the airline spared first-class passengers the risks of injury associated with maneuvering around a pesky beverage cart to get to the restroom.

She wiggled her butt on the padded chair and stuffed her purse under the seat. A side-eyed glance revealed that Mark was tapping his fingers on his tray table.

"I didn't sleep well last night. I'm sure I'll be out within minutes." She stretched her arms and yawned. "You won't even know I'm here."

Mark sighed. "Somehow I doubt that very much."

CHAPTER SIX

Mark watched Karen as she made her way to the plane's restroom. He wanted to block her image from his vision, but the sway of her hips pulled him in. Just before she disappeared through the tiny door, he realized what he was doing: moving his head from side to side, too—in perfect rhythm with her steps.

His reprieve from being tortured by her presence didn't last long enough. Minutes later, she returned to her seat. She'd taken off her jacket and wrapped its sleeves around her waist. The T-shirt she wore stretched across her chest, the look so enticing he nearly chewed the inside of his mouth to stop himself from making a rash move—like marching her back to the restroom so they could have sex at twenty-five-thousand feet. She'd never agree to a reckless liaison like that, but a guy and his fantasies were like a guy and his dick: where one went, the other most definitely followed.

He stood and let her pass. Kept his face blank, too, when her hands brushed against his waist as she maneuvered around him. Stopped himself from breathing the sweet scent that lingered in his space after she'd dropped into her seat. Batted away a few of her curls when she flipped her hair like an actress in a shampoo commercial. He predicted this would be a turbulent flight. For his libido.

Karen whipped out her e-reader, and he caught himself peeking at her digital library. The covers surprised him. There were bare chests everywhere. Lots of windswept hair and openmouthed kisses. Sexy as fuck. And not appreciated at this moment.

The innocent temptress caught him spying on her reading material and widened her eyes in excitement. "*Oooh,* this is a good one. The heroine's a mechanic and car detailer. The hero is a straitlaced businessman. She's jacked up his ride by mistake. Made it so he can barely recognize his prized sports car." Karen leaned into him and whispered, "And when he finds out what happened, he's furious. She is, too. Because he's such a jerk about it. But the sparks between them? Undeniable."

He leaned in, wanting to hear more.

"You can just tell the sex scenes are going to be explosive." She mimicked an explosion with her hands and voice.

He hadn't expected her to be so animated, so her overblown demonstration nearly propelled him out of his seat. To save face, he pretended to search for something under his ass as he patted the bottom cushion. "Sounds riveting. I didn't figure on you reading that kind of stuff."

"When I'm nervous or stressed, a solid romance is the perfect escape. A steady diet of medical textbooks isn't healthy. Even I know that. Not sure I'll read it on the flight, though. I'm exhausted." She glanced at him. "I sure could use a drink. To relax me, you know? You think they'll offer whiskey?"

It sounded like an innocent question, but he had no interest in engaging her on this topic. "You like whiskey?"

She grinned. "I've only had it once. You probably don't remember, but it was the night we met, actually."

He wanted to forget what she'd told him the night they'd met, but this conversation dredged it all back to the surface, where he wouldn't be able to ignore the way she'd made him feel. Refusing to take the bait, he shrugged. "Sorry. Much of that night is fuzzy to me. I only remember bits and pieces here and there. Like Ethan and Gracie's big news."

She tapped her index finger against the top of her right thigh. "Well, that's good. I might have said some things best left unsaid."

Do not let her see you sweat, Mark. "Like what?"

She stopped tapping and waved her hand. "Oh, nothing really. Let's forget about it."

Excellent. That was exactly what he wanted to hear. She didn't want to go there again with him. So now they could interact with each other as friends. Nothing more. Relieved, he took a cleansing breath and settled into his seat, ready to review the report his Human Resources Department had sent him.

Two minutes into the first page of the report, he stopped. Karen was fidgeting, shifting in her seat in search of a comfortable spot. When that appeared not to work, she rustled through her bag, setting random contents on the seat tray table. She turned to him and puckered her lips. He drew back, unable to figure out what she could possibly have in mind. She held up a tube of lipstick. "It's called *Kinda Sexy*. The lipstick shade, I mean. I'm thinking about wearing it for the wedding. What do you think? Too much?"

He swallowed and stared at her pink lips. It should have been called, *These Lips Are Made for Sucking*, really, but she'd probably pop him in his mouth if he spoke his mind. "It's nice."

She smiled and dug into her purse some more. Keys. Hand sanitizer. Condoms.

Christ. He had to do something. "You know what you need? Hot tea. That'll get you relaxed enough to sleep during the flight."

"That's a great idea, actually." She reached up and hit the attendant call button. Unnecessary, given that said attendant was two feet away, but today Karen seemed intent on stretching her body into eye-catching positions.

The flight attendant—Bethany according to her name tag—swept in to serve her. "Yes, ma'am. How may I help you?"

"I'd like a cup of hot tea, please, with a splash of rum."

The flight attendant nodded and switched her attention to Mark. "And you, sir?"

Just knock this woman out, so I can read my report in peace. "Nothing for me, thanks."

Bethany returned with the cup of tea, which Karen scooped up with enthusiastic hands. "Yummy. This is going to be *so good.*"

Was it just him or did her voice sound breathy?

He tried to ignore the sounds of her sipping her tea. Tried not to glance at her lips as she licked them. Pretended he couldn't hear her murmurs of appreciation. But the more he tried to block her out, the more he heard and noticed every move, every sound, every damn thing she did. Finally, *finally*, she placed the cup on the tray table and draped the airline-issued blanket over her body.

"All set to take a nap?" he asked.

"I am. Thanks. With any luck, I'll be asleep for the rest of the flight." She leaned against the window and closed her eyes. "Happy reading."

He returned his attention to the HR report, flipping through the document. When Karen shifted closer to him, he didn't think much of it. Minutes later, though, she rested her cheek on his shoulder and snuggled into him, her steady breathing signaling that she'd fallen asleep. There was no way he wouldn't smell her now. Dammit. He inhaled as covertly as he could and regretted it. She smelled like apples, or maybe peaches, but the scent was faint, which made him want to press his nose against her neck to get the full effect. He wouldn't make such an asinine move, of course, but he sure as hell was tempted.

His gaze traveled to her hands, both of which she'd tucked between her thighs. Her thumbs rested atop her jeans. She wore her nails short, filed in a square shape, shiny but clear. A vision of those hands wrapped around his cock flashed through his mind.

She mumbled something unintelligible, startling him out of his dirty daydream.

She moved her hand across his torso and slipped a single finger into the space between the middle two buttons of his shirt, one layer away from touching his skin. The rest of her hand lay on his stomach. He moved to wake her up but stopped himself. He didn't know why. He just did.

From there, his mind took over. So he closed his eyes and let it take him where it obviously wanted to go. If they were alone, his mind taunted, he'd move her hand to his cock and help her stroke him through his pants. She'd wake up then, groggy and disoriented, and her glassy eyes would go round with the realization of whom she was with and what she was doing. But she'd warm to the idea quickly, her soft lips parting and then curving into a seductive smile. Without a word between them, he'd pull her body up to straddle him. She'd lean over and kiss him. A tender exploration that would grow more heated as he stroked her hips and back.

From there, they'd move at a frantic pace, working together to remove the clothes separating them from the skin-on-skin contact they wanted. He'd remove her jeans. She'd unzip his pants, tugging at them until he rose off the seat and rolled down his boxer briefs. She'd stare at his cock, her eyes gleaming with appreciation, of course. With her hands on his shoulders, she'd center herself over him and slam down on his dick in one forceful motion. Fuck. That would feel so good.

"Excuse me, Mr. Lansing. Did you need anything?"

Mark opened his eyes and stared at the flight attendant. She faked a smile as she waited for his response.

Holy shit. *What the hell was he doing fantasizing about Karen while the woman slept next to him?* "No, no. I'm fine. Must have dozed off."

"*Right.* Well, if you need anything, please don't hesitate to let me know."

He faked a smile in return. "I won't. Thanks."

The flight attendant nodded and pivoted on her sensible pumps.

He shrugged his shoulder to wake up his seatmate. "*Psst.* Karen." "*Hmmm?*"

"Karen," he whispered. "I need to use the restroom."

She sprang away from him and opened her eyes wide, a faint blush appearing on her cheeks as she regained her bearings. "Sorry about that. Taking up your personal space, I mean. I'm a heavy sleeper."

He was grateful for that. If she had any idea what he'd been imagining while she lay against him, she'd deck him. He nodded and stood. "Not a problem, believe me. I was so engrossed in the report that it barely registered. You didn't disturb me at all." He moved out of the row, just in case lightning struck him in that instant; at the very least, he'd spare her.

The next hour of the flight passed without incident. They spoke briefly two times, once when he passed her a replenished drink and again to collect the small amount of garbage they'd accumulated on their tray tables. Still, Mark couldn't have been more hyperaware of her if he'd tried. And he was *really* trying not to be hyperaware of her.

He glanced at Karen, her head mere inches from her e-reader. It would have been so easy to slip his hand through hers and tug her to him, but he saw no point in starting something he would never finish. Karen represented everything he didn't want in a partner: too young, too inexperienced, and too unsettled. But denying that he was attracted to her would have been futile, too.

Both he and Karen planned to be permanent fixtures in Gracie's and Ethan's lives, which meant they had to find a way to interact with each other despite their inauspicious beginning. Their first encounter had been sparked by lust, by the heady feeling of mutual attraction. He'd never engaged her on an intellectual level, which meant he'd seen her only as a sexual being, a potential lover. The source of the problem came to him—as obvious as a neon sign flashing in front of his eyes. Even if he wanted to resist her, he'd set himself up to fail by having no other frame of reference for her as a person. It shamed him. A little. But it galvanized him, too.

He stuffed the report in his bag and turned to her. "You start medical school in the fall, right?"

Her head remained bent. "Yup."

"Are you excited? Anxious?"

She set her reading aside and stared at her hands. After releasing a deep sigh, she tucked one leg under the other, and twisted her torso in his direction. "Both. On the one hand, I'm blown away by the fact that I did it. *I* got into medical school. On the other hand, I wonder if I'm ready. Do I have the chops to do well?"

"But it's not that easy to get in. You need good grades, recommendations, excellent exam scores, I imagine. All of those indicators can't be wrong, can they?"

"Those indicators help predict the likelihood that you'll succeed in medical school, but they don't guarantee that you will."

"Of course they don't. There are no guarantees in life."

"Right. Of course. Just nervous about this next chapter in my life, I suppose."

"Have you always wanted to be a doctor?"

"Not always, no. I've always been interested in science, though. And it comes easy to me. My brain appreciates the structure of numbers and equations, so classes like chemistry and physics don't freak me out."

"I'm a numbers person, too. I went in a different direction, though, obviously. What led you to medicine?"

"I played soccer in high school. Got hurt one day. I wish I could say the injury happened in the middle of a championship game, but I broke my arm in practice, trying to defend a goal. We went to one of those urgent care centers." She smiled, a wistful expression on her face. "I'll never forget the nurse who helped me."

"Was she the one who inspired you to become a doctor?"

Her smile slipped. "No."

"What happened?"

"Oh, don't get me wrong. The nurse was great. Despite the place being understaffed and very busy, she answered all my questions. I was curious about everything. She explained to my parents what to expect. Consoled my mother, too. My mother was really beside herself. The nurse calmed her, told her everything would be okay. Then the doctor came in. And I became a body. He never once asked me if I had any questions. Addressed my dad, not my mom. At all. And left within forty-five seconds, to do more important things, I guess."

"You wanted to be a doctor who would do better under those circumstances."

"Exactly. Being a numbers person, I understand the appeal of dealing with just the facts. For the most part, that's how my brain works, too. But a doctor has such an important role in people's lives. Sometimes you have to take a step back, no matter what's going on in your professional and personal lives, and recognize that the individual you're speaking with is a real person and what you say matters to them. Some people say they always knew they wanted to be a doctor. That's not my story. But I grasp science easily, and I try to be a compassionate person, so why not me?"

He moved closer, touched by her words. "We need a million more like you, in my opinion."

Grinning as though she'd received her first compliment ever, she bumped him with her shoulder. "Well, I don't know about that, but thanks anyway."

She radiated energy and warmth—and a whole lot of sexy without even trying. How she did it, he didn't care to know. He raised his finger to play with a curl that had come loose from her ponytail.

The move turned into an awkward stretch, however, when he realized what he was about to do.

"You know, I'm glad Gracie and Ethan brought us together. I think we could become great friends," he said.

She'd been on the verge of leaning into him, probably because he'd given her every reason to believe he'd welcome the contact, but she drew back on his last word. Though he'd emphasized their new friendship to set boundaries for himself, he'd also hoped to send her a message, too. Her sudden interest in the contents of her purse confirmed that she'd heard that message loud and clear.

Mimi came out of nowhere, leaning into Karen and Mark's row—and breaking the uneasy moment. "That Marine is hot," she told Karen. "No wedding ring, either. I'd love to see him stand at attention, if you know what I mean. Oorah!"

Okay. There was only so much a man should be expected to take. He rose to stretch his legs, and Mimi plopped into his seat. Just as well, since he needed a minute to get his shit together.

He'd wanted to establish a connection with Karen based on something other than their mutual attraction. And he'd managed that in spades. Problem was, now he'd gotten a glimpse of her intelligence and compassion, too. And those traits made her infinitely *more* attractive to him, not less.

In a few hours, they'd be in Puerto Rico, where he'd stay for three days. Despite his attraction, surely he could resist her for three days. With the Marines' battle cry in mind, he prepared for battle. His mission: to fight his attraction to Karen at all costs. *Oorah.*

CHAPTER SEVEN

The man had mastered the art of confusing her. Trying to decipher his odd behavior would only be an exercise in frustration, so Karen vowed not to analyze any of it. She maintained that resolve on the terminal's moving walkway, up the stairs to ground transportation, and as she searched for their driver. Behind her, Mimi and Mark discussed the possibility of visiting El Yunque, a tropical rain forest on the northeastern part of island.

Blah, blah, blah. Yadda, yadda, yadda. Mark and Mimi's carefree chatter irritated her, and she had no idea why. Rising on her toes to see above the heads of the travelers bustling around her, she scanned the area for a sign with her name on it. When she failed to locate their driver, she stopped short and spun around, which caused her to collide with Mark, who'd been walking behind her. "*Oof,*" she said against his chest.

Mark whispered for her ears only. "Admit it. You have a thing for my chest."

Yes, I do.

She stepped back and shook her head. *No. No, I don't.*

See? Confusing. One minute he'd reached out to touch a strand of her hair. The next minute he'd claimed to be grateful for their new friendship. And now he'd made a suggestive comment about his chest. His big, solid chest.

Damn him. She did *not* need this now.

She drew back and gave him her best "not in this lifetime" smile. "In your dreams, Lansing." Then she linked her arm with Mimi's. "We need to find our driver."

Together, she and Mimi searched the crowd.

Her eyes finally found the sign that read, PENNINGTON AND RAMIREZ, and she waved to the driver who would take them the fifteen-minute drive from the airport to Hotel El Convento. As its namesake suggested, the hotel had once served as a convent. Gracie couldn't resist the hotel's old world charm, and its proximity to the numerous art museums in Old San Juan was an added benefit.

A tall man in a black suit and cap held a sign with Mark's last name on it. He must have made his own arrangements then. She turned to Mark and schooled her features. "Where are you staying?"

His eyes met hers. "The Ritz-Carlton."

Ah. Definitely more modern accommodations than hers. She'd never visited the Ritz, but she knew it was a favorite among international travelers who wanted the familiarity of a luxury chain.

"We'll see you in a few hours for dinner?" she asked.

"Sure. Take care, ladies."

"Bye," Mimi called out as she put on her sunglasses. Shoulder to shoulder, they watched Mark walk away. When he was out of earshot, Mimi whistled. "That man's ass is a force unto itself."

Distracted by the view, Karen blurted out the first thing that came to mind. "I like firm butts and I cannot lie."

Mimi stared at her in disbelief. "Wow. That man brings out a side of you I've never seen."

Unfortunately for Karen, she didn't know if that was a good or a bad thing.

* * *

Gracie had left Karen a welcome note at hotel check-in. Ethan had arranged a series of spa treatments for Gracie, the note explained, followed by a couple's massage for the bride and groom. They'd see everyone later that evening. Which meant Karen needed to hightail it to Abuela Marta's house to help prepare for the pre-wedding dinner.

Gracie had offered to plan a dinner at the hotel, but Abuela Marta had insisted that her home would be the perfect place for a small gathering of family and friends. Gracie had already pissed off their grandmother by choosing to stay in Old San Juan, but she'd justified the decision by emphasizing that, with only a few days to prepare, she and Ethan needed to stay close to the wedding venue. So when Abuela Marta had insisted on hosting the dinner, Gracie caved. Her sister's sense of self-preservation had clearly kicked in, because an annoyed Abuela Marta was *not* to be messed with.

Karen's cousin Alex picked her up at the hotel an hour later. He exited his compact Toyota and drew the attention of several woman waiting outside the lobby. She understood the appeal. Alex sported a short, military-style haircut that emphasized his sculpted cheekbones and hazel eyes. And she'd never seen him without his trademark smile, a lopsided affair that revealed annoyingly perfect teeth.

"Karen. Look at you. You're all grown up, college graduate," he said as he captured her in a bear hug. He moved to ruffle the hair on top of her head and caught himself. "Not a little girl anymore, huh?"

"Exactly."

"Just do me a favor while you're here," he said as he placed her carry-on suitcase in his trunk. "Take it easy. I don't want to have to kick some man's ass for looking at you the wrong way."

Alex had always been her favorite cousin. Three years older than her, he'd been protective of her since Karen and Gracie's first trip to the island. But back then he'd been concerned about the bullies.

She fiddled with the seat belt and strapped herself in. "Don't worry about me. I'll be on my best behavior during this trip."

He started the engine and waggled his eyebrows. "Best behavior is a relative term, *prima*."

"True enough, *primo*."

As he maneuvered his way through Old San Juan, Karen peppered him with questions, wanting to catch up on everything she'd missed. "How's your mom?"

Alex gripped the steering wheel and sighed. "She's fine. I think she wants to move out. She's been grumbling about needing her own space, but Abuela Marta can't understand why she'd take on the costs of her own place when Abuela Marta has two empty bedrooms. And now that the economy's shot to shit, who's to say Mom won't be out of a job soon. Anyway, that's their issue. I've got my own issues with my mom."

"Like what? Oh, wait. Let me guess. She wants you to settle down."

"Yes, at the ripe old age of twenty-five I'm apparently letting my good years go to waste."

This was a recurring theme in her family—Gracie had even battled with their parents about it—so Karen understood Alex's frustration. "Damn. That's harsh. But inquiring minds want to know, is there anyone special on the horizon?"

"I'm too young to be thinking about settling down. Besides, I doubt my mother would approve of anyone I chose to bring home."

"High standards?"

Alex scowled. "Let's just say she has outdated standards. And that's all I want to say about that. What about you? Anyone special?"

Karen studied his profile, many more questions on the tip of her tongue. She sensed that he wanted to deflect her attention away from his love life, however. Fair enough. She hadn't seen Alex in a few years, and although he was family, she didn't know much about his personal life. He might not be ready to talk to her about it now, but maybe if she opened up to him now, he'd feel comfortable doing the same in the future. "I didn't date much in college. Being premed kept me busy. I can't imagine starting a relationship in medical school, so it looks like I'll be unattached for a while."

"You don't sound happy about that."

"No, it's fine." Well, it had been fine until she'd met Mark. Now she didn't know what she wanted. "The thing is, I always assumed I wouldn't meet the love of my life in college because…"

Alex laughed. "Because college boys are idiots."

"Many of them, yes. My first-year roommate thought she'd met the love of her life at school. She came to the university like gangbusters, ready to excel in the business school. Kicking ass and taking names and all that. Next thing I knew she was pregnant and dropping out. Oh, and the love of her life disappeared after she told him about the baby. He transferred out of state, which apparently had been the plan all along."

Alex whistled and shook his head. "Damn, that's fucked up."

"Right? Gets me angry every time I think about it. So you can see why I wasn't too enthusiastic about dating in college. And now with med school bearing down on me, I can't see that dating anyone would make sense." She slipped her hands between her thighs and blew out a breath. Shit. This was hard to talk about. "But I have needs, too."

"We all do," Alex said.

"Exactly."

"But you don't have to date someone to have your needs met, Karen."

Karen's rebellious brain produced an image of Mark in her head. She slipped on her sunglasses, needing to shield her eyes from Alex's curious gaze. Yes, he had a point there.

* * *

Mark stepped out of the car, his gaze settling on Karen within seconds. She stood on the porch of her grandmother's house and was greeting guests. She'd pinned her hair on top of her head and let a few ringlets fall around her shoulders. The hairstyle gave him an unobstructed view of her neck and lovely collarbones, and the coral sundress she wore emphasized her slim waist and curvy hips. She'd worn a pretty outfit. Nothing more. Nothing less. But his traitorous brain tricked him into thinking she'd chosen the outfit with him in mind.

He managed to draw his gaze away from Karen and surveyed the neighborhood. Rows of concrete houses with red-tile roofs dotted the streets, each one battling the others for the title of house with the most eye-catching color scheme: sky blue and green, canary yellow and white, and a rust color that either had been selected on purpose or represented abnormal wear and tear. Green grass and lush palm trees fronted some of the homes.

Abuela Marta's house boasted an outdoor staircase that led to a second-floor balcony. The concrete walls of the home had been painted pink and white, and the white picket fence jutted from the right side of the house, wrapped around the porch, and ended at the carport on the house's left side. If the house had had any curves, it would pass for a giant flamingo.

He would have preferred to walk past Karen, because engaging in as little conversation with her as possible seemed the safe thing to do, but the thought of ignoring her altogether bothered him more than the risk of succumbing to her charms.

"Hello, Karen."

Her smile faltered as she turned to face him. "Good to see you again, Mark."

They stared at each other. *Would it always be like this between them?* This tightness in the air stifling them? The sense that what they really wanted to say or do bubbled under the surface? He hoped not—for both their sakes. "Same here." He dug his hands in his pockets and gave her an inquiring look.

She straightened and shook her head as if to clear it. "Oh, right. Go ahead inside. Ethan and Gracie are holding court. When you have a minute, I'll introduce you to my grandmother." She moved closer and stood on her toes to whisper in his ear. "She's a spitfire. Be careful."

He smiled and crossed the threshold. Heat smacked him in the face, along with the smell of unfamiliar foods. He sniffed the air. Just past the foyer two tables of food in various chafing and serving dishes made his mouth water. Guests milled about with plates in their hands, alternating between eating the sumptuous food and catching up with friends. Salsa music played in the background.

He found Gracie and Ethan in the living room.

His friend squeezed his shoulder and clasped his hand. "Hey, buddy. Glad you could make it." Ethan turned to Gracie. "Now we can get married."

Gracie raised a brow. "Sorry to tell you this, Mark, but we would have gotten married without you. Still, I'm glad you're here."

"She's nothing if not honest, eh?" he said to Ethan.

"And beautiful. And smart." Ethan dipped his head and nuzzled Gracie's neck. "And sexy. Let's not forget sexy."

"Down, boy," Mimi shouted from across the room. She pinned him with her stare, and then she mouthed, *I'm watching you.*

Ethan groaned. "Did you put her up to this?" he asked Gracie.

Gracie laughed. "What kind of question is that? Does anyone ever have to put Mimi up to anything?"

"No, I suppose not," Ethan replied.

A group of women laughing in the corner drew his attention. At the center of their circle stood a man around his age. The women hung on his every word—and he appeared to have plenty of words to share.

Mimi brushed against him. "That's Daniel," she said with a sneer. "Friend of the family and wannabe Casanova."

"Be nice, Mimi," Gracie said.

"I'm not sure I know how," Mimi replied without a hint of amusement on her face.

Unfortunately for Daniel, he chose that moment to join their small gathering. "Gracie, Ethan. Congratulations. I'm happy for you."

Gracie greeted Daniel enthusiastically. Ethan? Not so much.

Mimi even less so. "Daniel, how can you handle all the adoration? The player in you must be in his element."

Daniel fingered a lock of Mimi's blond hair. "Tell me this, Mimi. Is it frustrating when people make assumptions about you because of your looks? Because of the sound of your voice? Because of that slight Southern accent you work so hard to disguise?"

Mimi's pale skin blushed a furious red, but her blue eyes flashed with anger. "Changing the subject. Definitely a skill well within your wheelhouse, I see."

Daniel chuckled, seemingly unconcerned with the fire in Mimi's eyes. "I could say the same about your talent for unnecessary rudeness."

Gracie's head snapped back. Ethan widened his eyes in shock And Mark dropped his head and stared at his watch. *Well, damn.*

Oblivious to the tension between Daniel and Mimi, Karen joined them, a clean plate in her hand. "I'm going to stuff my face. Mark, would you like me to give you a rundown of the dishes?"

No. Not really. He imagined her "rundown." With his luck, she'd use words like *tender, rich,* and *succulent.* Oh, and *moist.* He couldn't forget *moist.* She'd have him panting within seconds. But since he wanted no part of the boxing match between Daniel and Mimi, he nodded and got the hell out of there.

Minutes later, he marveled at the heaping plate of food in his hands. Karen had, in fact, used some of the words he'd imagined she would use—except for *succulent*. That word only sparked his own imagination apparently.

She inspected his plate and snapped her fingers. "You don't have rice. No Puerto Rican meal is complete without rice. That's in the kitchen. You should just go in there and help yourself. My grandmother makes a giant vat of it, in a pot the size of a witch's cauldron, and no one ever bothers to haul it into the dining room."

He held the overfull plate in his hand and listened to the sounds of silverware clattering in the kitchen. Laughter and music mixed with the bustle of still more food preparations. "I'll follow you, if you don't mind."

Her deep brown eyes shone, and she cracked a smile. "They won't bite, you know. My grandmother's a spitfire, but she's sweet, too. C'mon. Stay behind me and keep your gaze on the ground. No sudden movements."

"What are we? Paratroopers?"

She laughed. "I'm just kidding, Mark. Relax."

Older women moved at a frantic pace in the kitchen—stirring sauces, tasting each other's concoctions, and handing each other items in assembly-line fashion. One woman, however, leaned against the sink and gestured with her hands as she spoke rapid-fire Spanish. He guessed she was Karen's grandmother. He also guessed the matriarch of the family gave orders, and the others happily did her bidding. They all looked happy.

In the corner, a middle-aged couple laughed and danced to the music. He took in their features and coloring and made the connection: Gracie and Karen's parents—they had to be.

Karen's grandmother pushed her butt off the sink and shuffled toward them. She lifted her chin in his direction. "*Quien es el?*" she asked Karen.

"Abuela, this is Mark. *El mejor amigo de Ethan.*" She turned to him to translate. "Ethan's best friend."

Understanding dawned on Abuela Marta's face.

Mark held out a hand. "*Mucho gusto,*" he said in an attempt to speak her native language.

"Good to meet you, too," Abuela Marta replied with a wink. To Karen, she said, "*Muy guapo*, no?"

Karen widened her eyes and laughed. "*Sí*, Abuelita, *él es guapisimo.*"

Karen's father strolled across his room, his outstretched hand and a friendly smile immediately putting Mark at ease. "Good to meet you, Mark. I'm Hector Ramirez, Karen and Gracie's father. That lovely woman over there is my wife, Lydia."

Lydia waved from across the room.

Hector turned to his mother and wrapped an arm around her shoulder. "Now, as for you, please leave the poor man alone. He's a friend of the family now."

Abuela Marta removed Hector's arm and swatted him. "Don't tell me what to do. I'm still your mother. If I need to remove a *chancla* and take you over my knee, I will."

Hector sprinted across the room and hid behind his wife. "It's not just you, Mark," he said with a smile. "She's like this with everyone. I'm a grown man and she's still threatening to beat me with her flip-flops."

Karen motioned for Mark to join her at the stove. After placing a few spoonfuls of rice on her own plate, she scooped a huge helping onto his. "*Now* you're ready. C'mon, we can eat in the living room."

They found two empty chairs. Karen unfolded her napkin and crossed her legs at the knee.

He took a peek, admiring her smooth legs.

"Have you had Puerto Rican food before?" she asked.

"Can't say that I have."

"Okay. Start with the *pernil.*"

"What's that?"

"It's roasted pork shoulder. Without it, no Puerto Rican family celebration is complete."

He bit into the pork and moaned. "Oh, this is fantastic. I love garlic, and this tastes like it's slathered in it."

"It is. And it's marinated overnight. That's what helps make it so moist." With her head bowed, she moved the food on her plate around. After a few seconds of silence, she raised her head. "Hey, if you're not doing anything tomorrow afternoon, after the dress rehearsal, I can take you to the beach. It's relatively close to Old San Juan. If you want authentic Puerto Rican food, the kiosks by the beach are your best bet. Besides someone's kitchen, of course."

He studied his plate and scrambled for a reason not to accept her invitation. "That would be great, but I have to get some work done while I'm here. Tomorrow will be busy for me." That excuse sounded thin even to his own ears.

"Sure, sure. I understand. Not a big deal. Just thought I'd offer." Before he could change his mind, she rose. "Excuse me. I see someone I should say hello to. Enjoy the meal."

She strode across the room and set her plate on a nearby table. Then she fell into the arms of a really good-looking guy whose astonished reaction didn't last long. Within seconds, he returned her hug and kissed her on the cheek.

And damned if that didn't annoy Mark. He had no right to feel anything at all. Had sent every conceivable signal to let her know he didn't want to explore a relationship with her. But right now, his mischievous brain was playing devil's advocate. Maybe she'd extended the offer precisely because she, too, wanted to be friends. In which case, what real harm could come from accepting her invitation? In fact, hanging out with her on friendly terms might be the perfect antidote to his interest.

Karen lifted her plate from the table and fed the young guy a forkful of food. With a wink, she took her napkin and dabbed his lips. Mark had no control of the legs that moved straight in Karen's direction.

"Karen."

She spun toward him, fork still in hand. "Yes?"

"If that invitation still stands, I'd like to accept. I'd love to go to the beach with you tomorrow afternoon."

Karen regarded him in silence, a puzzled expression on her face.

The good-looking guy held out his hand. "My name's Alex. I'm Karen's cousin. You are?"

Karen broke out of her trance. "Sorry. This is Mark, Ethan's best friend."

"Good to meet you, Alex."

Alex smiled. "Ah. Are you getting your needs met tomorrow, Karen?"

She jabbed Alex in the side with her elbow. "So funny, Alex."

"I try to be," Alex said.

"You're failing," Karen replied.

Mark watched their exchange like a spectator at a tennis match.

The air of familiarity between the cousins now made sense. "So we'll head out after the wedding rehearsal?" he asked Karen.

"Sure."

Her smile erased any lingering doubt about his decision. "Great."

"Great," she echoed.

Alex cleared his throat. "Well, since you're both great, I'll leave you to your greatness."

Karen stared at Alex's retreating back. "He's my cousin, and the big brother I never had," she told him. "Takes the pain in the ass part of his brotherly duties a little too seriously."

"No worries. He seems like a good guy. So tomorrow should be fun. I'm looking forward to it."

A faint blush appeared on her cheeks. "So am I."

He itched to caress her face. Her smooth skin practically begged for it. But friends didn't caress each other's cheeks—facial or *otherwise*—so he held himself back. "Let's be sure to exchange numbers before I leave, okay?"

"Sure," she said.

He walked away in search of Ethan.

Tomorrow he and Karen would spend an hour or so at the beach. An outing between friends. After that, their last day in Puerto Rico would be filled with wedding activities, making it unlikely that they'd have much time to spend alone together. So all he had to do was get through tomorrow, and then he'd be home free.

CHAPTER EIGHT

Karen shook her head as Mark led her toward the car. "A black sedan with windows? We're going to the beach, Mark. To hang out. Everyone's going to think we're security detail for a VIP."

As he held the car door open, Mark focused on Karen's face, making sure his gaze didn't land on her body. "Why won't they assume we're the VIPs?"

"Um. I'm wearing cut-off jeans and you're wearing cargo shorts. I don't *look* like a very important person."

Now that she'd mentioned her shorts, he couldn't help appreciating the way the frayed edges rested on her tanned thighs. Thighs he very easily pictured wrapped around his…Nope. He refused to go there.

"I beg to differ," he said. "And these are board shorts, thank you very much. Anyway, I've hired the car service for the duration of the trip. Why would I let it go to waste?"

"Aren't you worried about drawing attention to yourself?"

He peered at her behind his aviator sunglasses. "Should I be worried?"

"I have no idea. I don't make a regular habit of hanging out with wealthy men."

He took her hand and squeezed it. "Our driver has experience working security detail. I didn't hire him for that purpose, but the guy is huge. I'm pretty sure he'd back me up if anything went down. Trust me on this. We'll be fine."

He lifted her chin and willed her to look at him. "Okay?" he asked.

His touch was more intimate than he'd intended, and more than she'd expected if her flushed cheeks were any guide.

"Okay," she said without meeting his gaze, and then she scrambled into the car. Her cheeks burned.

After he'd settled in beside her, Mark signaled the driver, and the sedan eased into traffic.

"Okay. Fess up. How are you and Ethan spending his last evening of freedom?"

"I don't think Ethan views marriage to Gracie as a loss of freedom. But to answer your question, nothing too exciting. We're going to the casino at the Ritz."

She didn't hide the skepticism in her voice. "Really. That's all?"

He lifted his eyebrows and lowered his sunglasses to stare at her. "Yes, *that's all*. What did you expect?"

"I'm not sure what I expected, but the possibility of a guys' night at the casino had never entered her mind. That sounds…civilized."

"How fitting. We're civilized men, after all."

She rolled her eyes. "Of course you are."

"The sarcasm is noted, Ms. Ramirez. Anyway, I should ask you the same question. What are you, Gracie, and Mimi doing tonight?"

"Gracie has requested an in-room massage, in-room dining, and a movie marathon."

"That sounds nice. I think I'll ditch Ethan and join you."

"That's the plan at least, but Mimi's been spending time with that Marine she met on the plane, so it might just be Gracie and me."

"I don't know Mimi well, but I highly doubt she'd miss your mini-bachelorette party. She strikes me as a loyal friend."

"No, you're right. She wouldn't miss it. But I'll admit that the idea of spending time alone with Gracie would be just as great. I mean, Mimi's a blast, but it's different when she's around. She's loud and likes to be the center of attention. My gut tells me Gracie's going to be focused on a little introspection tonight. Mimi won't necessarily be conducive to that."

"Maybe she'll surprise you." He thought back to that uncomfortable moment between Mimi and Daniel at the pre-wedding dinner. "There's a reason she and Gracie are so close, right? I doubt Mimi is always fun and games. No person can be like that one hundred percent of the time."

She stared out the car window, her face suggesting she was lost in thought. "That's a fair point."

Minutes later, they arrived at the beach. With nowhere to park the car, Mark sent the driver on his way and promised to call him when they needed to be picked up again.

After he'd taken a few steps in the sand, Mark stopped and stared out at the clear and calm waters. "Wow. This is breathtaking."

Beside him, Karen shielded her face against the sun and smiled. "Yeah. My earliest memories of visiting Puerto Rico begin here. Our family loved this beach. It's where the locals go, far away from the touristy beaches in places like Condado." She removed her sandals and held them in one hand. "Want to dip your feet in?"

He kicked off his sandals. "I do."

They walked to the water's edge. Karen stuck a toe in the water and sprang back. "Too cold."

He whipped around and tried to splash her with his feet. "Nonsense. This is perfect."

She returned to the water's edge and tiptoed into the water. "*Brrr.* I don't care what you say. It's cold. But I'll get used to it. C'mon. There's a kiosk about a quarter mile down the beach. We can grab a snack there."

They walked along the shore, their progress slowed by the wet sand and the occasional wave breaking at their feet. With one hand holding her hair back against the wind, Karen pointed out places she and her family had frequented during their summer vacations, and she divulged another secret: She'd learned to swim when she was nine, after a near-drowning incident at this very beach.

"Are you afraid of the water now?" he asked.

"A little. I'll put my feet in the water, but I haven't taken a swim in over a decade."

"Maybe one day I'll convince you to wade in with me."

Without a hint of sarcasm in her voice, she rejected that idea out of hand. "Not going to happen."

The kiosk came into view, the center of a social gathering the likes of which he'd never seen in a beach setting. Adults and children, some in swimwear and others casually dressed, ate and socialized in groups. To the right of the kiosk, employees of a makeshift produce market disassembled the display of fresh fruits and vegetables, carrying them away in large wooden crates. Dusky yellow lamplights turned on as the sun set in the distance. Several sets of multicolored bulbs, like the ones his dad had strung on their small Christmas tree each year, dotted the edges of the square. In one corner, a group of old men slammed down their dominoes with authority, chuckling as they tried to outdo one another's performances. He could get used to this.

Karen trotted off to grab a few "snacks." She returned to the table with a full smile. That smile eased the tension in his own body. His stomach didn't get tied in knots at the sight of her. No, what she did to him was much worse. She soothed him. Made him calm. Calm enough to enjoy her company and relax in his own skin. A dangerous state given that he wanted to keep his distance.

They claimed a small cast-iron table near the kiosk. With a playful flourish, she handed him a piece of dough wrapped in a white paper napkin. "Here. Try an *alcappuria*."

"What is it?"

"It's a fritter." She sank her teeth into her own *alcapurria* and dabbed her napkin across her chin. "Mmmm. Fried yummy goodness."

He stared at her lips as he asked the next question. "What's in it?"

"Ground beef. Green plantains. *Yautia*."

"Yau-what?"

"*Yautia*. It's a root vegetable." She snapped her fingers, searching for the word in English. "Taro root."

"The English translation means nothing to me." He inspected it from several angles, as though he were examining a precious gem for flaws. "Huh. I'm sure you've heard this before, but this looks incredibly phallic."

She nudged his shoulder, a faint blush appearing on her sun-kissed cheeks. "C'mon, just eat it."

He scrunched his nose and regarded the *alcapurria* with suspicion. "Now there's an effective pitch for you. This thing that looks like your penis? Just eat it."

"You're stalling, Lansing."

"You're right. I am. Okay, here goes." He bit into the fritter and raised his eyebrows. "It's good," he managed to say in between chews. "Really good."

"Told you. Now you have to wash it down with Malta."

"*Aaaaand* that's where you've lost me. I've tried Malta in the states. What's the point of having a malted beverage without alcohol? None. Same reason I never drink decaf."

She dropped her head in a show of good-natured exasperation. Then she straightened, her brown eyes twinkling. "Would you like me to order you a *beer* then?"

He took his last bite of the fritter, stood, and straightened his pants. "I'll take care of it. Need anything?"

"Nope. I'm enjoying my Malta."

The air clung to Mark's skin as he strode to the counter. A guitarist perched on a wooden crate played a slow song, the lazy tune a perfect accompaniment to the island's balmy weather. The server was busy attending to another patron, so Mark dropped onto a stool and watched the musician's nimble fingers strum the guitar.

A light and desperately needed breeze shook the multicolored bulbs strung along the posts at the four corners of the small square. He fell back in time, the glint of the lights reminding him of the plastic Christmas tree his father had decorated each year. Not a single holiday season passed without Mark asking why they couldn't have a live tree. And his father always gave the same answer: Because there was no point in investing in something that wasn't going to last. The predictable exchange always ended with a look between them, one acknowledging that his father's words referred not to the Christmas tree, but to an altogether different void in their lives.

A loud crash made him jump off the stool. To his right, the group of men who'd been playing dominoes shouted and surrounded a man who held his hands to his throat, a bluish tinge creeping up his puffy face. He'd upended his chair as he stood and gasped for air.

"Shit," Mark murmured to himself, unsure what to do. "He's choking."

Karen ran to the man and shouted for everyone to give him space. The men scrambled backward and she took over. "*Puedes hablar?*" she asked the man. Based on Mark's rudimentary command of the Spanish language, he guessed she'd asked the man whether he was able to speak.

The man shook his head and clutched at his throat. Karen stood behind him and wrapped her arms around his thick waist, centering her hands just below his belly button. Sweat trickled down his skin and panic set in his eyes. Karen pressed her hands against his abdomen, only the top of her head visible above the man's shoulders. After several thrusts, the man coughed something up. Mark had never been so happy to see a piece of masticated meat. Gross? Certainly. But that mangled meat reminded him of the gravity of the situation: A few minutes more without oxygen and that man might have suffered brain damage.

Karen pointed a finger in the air and directed the man to follow it. After several questions and answers in Spanish, the man hugged Karen and repeated "*Gracias*" to her.

Did men swoon? Because that had been the hottest display of

badassery he'd ever seen—and her command of the situation made his knees weak.

After chatting with a few of the bystanders, she hurried past him, her hands resting on her hips and her gait reminiscent of someone who'd just finished running a race. He trailed after her, sensing she needed time and space to regroup. She trudged through the sand with her head down. When she reached the water, she bent at the waist to catch her breath.

"What you did back there was amazing," he said behind her.

She straightened and gulped in air. "Thanks."

"I think you've found your calling."

She lifted a brow. "I didn't perform life-saving surgery on the man. I did the Heimlich. You don't need a medical degree for that."

"No, but you took control of the situation, and you comforted him after a bad scare. Not everyone has the ability to do those things. You did them as if they were second nature to you."

"Yeah. I didn't have time to think about the what-ifs. I was on autopilot."

"I think we should celebrate your heroic efforts."

She crinkled her nose in disbelief. "Oh, yeah. How?"

"By getting in the water."

Her eyebrows shot up. "No."

"C'mon. I'll go with you."

"No."

"Fine. Suit yourself." He took off his shirt and dropped it on the sand. "Be right back."

Manipulative? Sure it was. Would it work? He'd find out soon enough.

* * *

Wait. Hold the phone. He had a tattoo?

Karen's eyes devoured the view of Mark's back as he waded into the water. The tattoo sat in the center of his lower back, in the dip just above his impressive butt. She wasn't sure, but it looked like an infinity symbol. Given Mark's fascination with numbers, the choice didn't surprise her. But the fact that he had one? That *definitely* surprised her.

His back muscles rippled as he swung his arms over his head and stretched. To make matters more torturous, he turned back and waved, a bright smile lighting up his face. After she returned his wave, he scooped a handful of water, drew it over his head, and released it onto his face and shoulders.

He was on a beach, in the water, his gorgeous body backlit by the sunset behind him. A freakin' man-nymph. This was an opportunity she couldn't pass up, no matter how squeamish the sea made her. So she tamped down her nervousness and headed straight to him. And if she needed his shirtless body for support, he'd understand, right?

She waded in until the water covered her ankles. Okay, that wasn't so bad.

Mark returned to shore and held out his hand. "Come on. You're doing great. And we won't go very far."

"Oh, I *know* we won't be going very far. And besides, unlike you, I didn't come prepared for an evening swim."

He splashed her legs. "You'll have to get your thighs wet at least."

"I'm dealing with long-repressed memories of a near-drowning, and this is the best you can come up with?"

Bent at the waist, he stopped splashing her and shook the water off his hands. "I'm sorry. You're right." He held out his arms. "Here. Hold on to me. I've got you."

Teeth chattering, she burrowed into his chest. "It's not as bad as I thought it would be, but it's so cold."

He wrapped his arms around her and held her tight. "You doing okay?"

She looked up at him then. "I'm fine." And that was true. "Thanks for getting me in the water."

"You're welcome. To be honest, I don't think there's much you can't do if you set your mind to it."

"I appreciate the vote of confidence," she murmured against him.

Her lips grazed his chest, and he stopped rubbing her arms. She affected him. That much she knew. He affected her, too. But she couldn't afford to be distracted by him, so she didn't acknowledge the accidental touch and enjoyed the view of the ocean instead. The waves rose and fell in an even tempo that lulled her into a state of calm.

He loosened his hold on her. "Still okay?" he asked softly.

She looked up and stared into his eyes, mesmerized by the way the water had spiked his thick eyelashes. "Yes."

His lips parted. Perhaps in silent invitation. She imagined her lips pressed against his and gathered the courage to ignore the consequences of what she was contemplating. The sand beneath her feet shifted as she rose on her toes. Just a kiss. That's all she needed or wanted. But then she saw it: a wave that likely reached Mark's shoulders, which meant it would certainly surpass hers. Karen's heart raced, and her stomach knotted in protest. *Oh, shit. Oh, shit. Oh, shit.* She turned and hightailed her ass out of the water, a graceless mess of flailing arms and legs.

She'd run so fast she could hardly catch her breath. Panting, she turned just in time to watch Mark emerge from the water. The wave had drenched him, but he didn't seem put out by that fact.

He reached her in seconds. "Take a deep breath, Karen. You're safe."

She was safe, but she wasn't well. She gulped in air, her frayed nerves refusing to settle down. Her stomach roiled as she tried to even out her breathing. It was no use, though. Unable to contain her nausea any longer, she bent at the waist and vomited at his feet.

Karen squeezed her eyes shut. *I wish I were home. I wish I were home.* If clicking her feet would have done any good, she'd have done that, too. Great. Just great. Cock-blocked by a freaking wave. But it was just as well. She had no business tempting herself with the likes of Mark Lansing.

CHAPTER NINE

For a solid ten minutes, Karen had considered wearing sunglasses to the wedding. She needed something—anything—to help her hide from the embarrassment of yesterday's debacle. Mark had been a good sport about it, of course, but the odds of her being able to look him in the eye after she'd upchucked next to his Italian leather sandals looked bleak. Which made his arrival at the wedding venue bittersweet.

The man wore a suit well. He'd opted not to wear a tie, choosing instead to leave the top two buttons of his dress shirt unbuttoned. Even from here, she could see the outline of his thighs each time he took a step. And when he settled his frame next to Ethan on the lawn, he placed his hands in his pockets, causing the fabric of his pants to stretch across his crotch. *Definitely a mountain. No molehill there.*

She knew now that despite his impeccably groomed exterior, Mark could be playful, too. She imagined he'd be the kind of man who'd screw you against a wall with his intense eyes boring into yours and then joke with you about how you almost broke him the minute he pulled out. And this was not the most appropriate place for her to picture all that in her head. *Damn. Just. Damn.* Luckily, a quick glance at Abuela Marta rid her of her naughty thoughts.

Karen took her position at the edge of the gazebo. The wedding planners had staked out a grassy area several hundred feet away from the visitors' entrance to Castillo de San Felipe del Morro, or El Morro as it was referred to by the islanders. The vast lawn generally provided no shade, but Gracie had arranged for the ceremony site to be covered by cream-colored canopies with ivy entwined around their posts.

Karen glanced at Mark's face as he surveyed the expanse of land and buildings that made up the almost five-hundred-year-old fort. His eyes darted from structure to structure, finally settling on the restored lighthouse near the fort's tip. Just beyond the lighthouse, the bottom of the fort's walls, in some places over one hundred and forty feet high, met the deep blue waters of San Juan Bay.

"It's breathtaking," Mark said.

Karen wrestled with her hair, which had lost its battle with both the humidity and the breezes coming off the bay as soon as the wedding guests had begun to trickle in. "I couldn't agree with you more. It's a perfect blend of culture, history, and nature."

"And if that weren't enough to defend the island, this heat will scorch your ass to smithereens, too."

Karen smiled. Several strands of her wayward hair stuck to the back of her neck, unable to hold the loose waves she'd spent so much time perfecting that morning. "Yes, there's that, too."

Beside them, Ethan alternated between eyeing the sky, checking his watch, and surveying the cobblestoned streets that led to the lawn. Mimi stood on the outskirts of the gathering and chatted with one of Karen's male cousins.

Mark shifted closer to Ethan. "You ready, E?"

Ethan shoved his hands into his black tuxedo. "I'm ready. Not even a speck of doubt in my mind, and that's some heady shit. I can't wait to see her."

When Karen heard Ethan's words, her eyes watered. Ethan's love for her sister made her happy—and inspired a touch of envy as well. What would it be like to be loved by someone so convinced that you were their "one"? *The one.* No man had ever been devoted to Karen in the way Ethan was devoted to her sister.

Mark's voice interrupted her thoughts. "Here she comes."

A stately limousine came into view. Her parents exited first, followed by the officiant. Their father turned and reached out for Gracie's hand.

Karen whipped her head in Ethan's direction, just in time to witness his audible intake of breath. The photographer swooped in to capture the moment when the groom first laid eyes on his bride. Mark leaned in and whispered something to Ethan that made him smile. Mimi, meanwhile, rushed over to take her place next to Karen.

Gracie, flanked by her parents, walked toward her groom. Her face couldn't have been any brighter; her smile couldn't have been any more joyful. She only had eyes for Ethan, and Ethan was so focused on his bride that Karen watched for signs that he was actually blinking.

Gracie wore a simple cream silk-organza gown, the ends of which floated around her ankles. Her hair, styled in a seemingly effortless side bun that had taken her stylist a few hours to achieve, complemented her vintage veil, the very same veil their mother had worn for her own wedding three decades ago.

As Gracie approached the arch, Karen saw Abuela Marta dabbing her eyes with a kerchief. Even her tough-as-granite grandmother couldn't hold back her emotions in the face of so much beauty.

Gracie's parents kissed and hugged her before Ethan took her hand. From that point, they walked together, and then they faced the officiant. After the officiant had greeted the guests, he informed them that Ethan and Gracie wanted to share a few words before they exchanged their vows.

The bride and groom faced each other and held hands. Ethan spoke first.

"The morning of my sister's wedding, I asked her, 'Em, how'd you know you were making the right decision? How'd you know he was the one?' She looked at me with a wistful expression and said, 'When you no longer need to ask that question, when the decision becomes as certain as your next breath, that's when you'll know.'" And as much as I hate to admit when my baby sis is right, I can't deny the truth of those words, because that's how I feel about our love, Gracie. It's a foregone conclusion. As certain as my next breath. A truth I neither can nor want to deny. You don't make me strive to be a better person. I *am* a better person now that you're in my life."

Gracie's eyes watered. Couples moved closer together. A child in the second row—Ethan's niece, she believed—made a show of gagging at Ethan's sentimental words.

Gracie took a deep breath and exhaled. "Love isn't calculated. It never comes to you by design. Often it catches you by surprise. I never dreamed I'd find someone who believes in me in the way you do. I never dreamed I'd find someone who doesn't want to change me. I never dreamed I'd find someone who thinks about my happiness before his. So in many ways, you see, today isn't a dream come true. It's much more than that, because you've given me the love I never dreamed of and so much more."

Karen wanted the same. Someday. Someday far, far away.

* * *

The reception ballroom, with its black-and-white-checkered floor, featured old world flair and a touch of modern ambience. Gracie and Ethan stood on a small balcony overlooking the dance floor, a photographer at the couple's side.

A twelve-piece band, which only moments ago had played a lazy jazz song, picked up the tempo.

"*Vamos a bailar!*" the lead singer called out. "We're gonna dance!" He cupped his ear to the audience. "I say *baila*, you say, *wepa!*" He pointed to the crowd. "*Baila!*"

"*Wepa!*" the guests cheered.

Guests sprang from their chairs and rushed to the small dance floor to join the fun.

With only fifty or so guests at the reception, Mark spotted Karen easily. Once again, she'd piled her hair on top of her head, leaving a few ringlets to cascade along her neck and back. She danced with one of her cousins. Well, Mark hoped he was a cousin, but then the man's hand slid from her shoulder to her waist and he gave her a seedy wink. Not a relative, then. And it didn't matter. Really. As soon as the reception ended, he'd head back to his suite, far away from Karen and the charm of Old San Juan.

He nursed his drink, intermittently taking big gulps and savoring the bitter bite of alcohol. He stopped himself from finishing it, knowing he needed his faculties to give the best man's speech.

His face partially hidden by the rim of his tumbler, he watched Karen weave her way through the guests. She smiled at him and reached for his hand. "C'mon, Lansing. You can't leave Puerto Rico until you've danced salsa."

Shit. How was he supposed to keep his distance while his hands rested on her waist? And as she shook her hips, no less?

He set the tumbler on a passing server's tray, but he hesitated to grab her hand. Her smile disappeared, leaving an expression of wariness in its wake. As he contemplated his next move, she swung her arms around her back and pivoted to leave.

What the hell was wrong with him? He could handle a fucking dance. Well, his dancing prowess was questionable, but he could survive a dance with her, if only so he didn't have to watch her shuffle back to the other side of the ballroom like a girl rejected by a silly boy at her first middle school dance. He reached out and touched the back of her arm. "Wait. You'll have to teach me."

She spun around, and her eyes lit up. "I'd love to."

They walked together and found a spot on the dance floor. She helped him place one of his hands on her shoulder blade. Being the suave man that he was, he stumbled as she adjusted them into the right position. She moved closer, staring into his eyes, and then she brought his other hand to her waist. "Usually, we'd hold our hands outstretched, but I think this will be easier."

He gulped and stared right back. But they didn't move, and then the band began a new song, this one eliciting universal approval from the crowd.

"Popular song?" he asked.

"Oh, yes. This is El Gran Combo. A beloved Puerto Rican Salsa band."

"What are they saying?"

"'*Brujeria*' is the name of the song." She licked her lips and pressed her body against his, maneuvering them into the correct position. "She's bewitched him. A *bruja* is a witch." She stepped back. "Now, to make this work, watch my feet."

Still holding on to her, he created space between them and watched her feet in the spiky sandals she wore.

"It's a simple motion. Move your left foot forward, and then switch your weight, so that you can move your right foot back."

He tried to copy her movements, but he failed to achieve the same result. "Wait. What was that you just did? You kicked out your foot. And you paused."

She snorted. "Don't worry about kicking your foot out. You're not ready for that."

He tried again.

"Yes, that's it. Be sure to swing your hips; they'll move naturally with your footwork."

"*Your* hips move naturally with the footwork. Mine? Not so much."

"You're doing great, Mark. Just do what feels good to you."

Right about now something else entirely would feel good to him.

After tripping on his own feet a few times, he eased into a comfortable pattern, his feet mirroring her footwork as well as could be expected.

Karen looked up at him, her radiant smile revealing the dimples in her sun-kissed cheeks. "Ready to spin me?"

"Nope, I'm good."

"C'mon, Mark, have faith in yourself. What's the worst that could happen?"

"I spin you so hard and fast that you tumble into a table?"

"Have faith in *me*, then. I promise I won't let you hurt me."

"All right. If that's what you want, you can't claim later that I didn't warn you."

She swung his hand above them and spun herself around, which would have been fine if she hadn't ended the spin with her butt pressed against his crotch. She turned her head to the side, and her cheek brushed against his chest. "See there? No one got hurt, right?"

His balls disagreed. They hurt. And tonight, they'd be blue. So very blue.

He dropped his head, pressing his face against her neck. Not an advisable move, but he couldn't help himself. Maybe the song itself had powers: the power to ensure that any man who danced with a woman would be entranced by her.

A weathered hand opened a wedge between them. "*Basta!*" Abuela Marta exclaimed through gritted teeth. "What are you do- ing? This is a wedding. *Ahora no es el momento para el baile sucio.*"

He didn't have to understand Spanish to know Abuela Marta didn't appreciate how he and Karen were dancing. Well, he didn't like it either.

Karen took Abuela Marta's hand. "*Lo siento, Abuelita*, but it's not dirty dancing." She shimmied her shoulders. "Just a little sexy, sexy."

Abuela Marta harrumphed and shimmied right back. "Well, too much of that and soon you'll have little babies, babies." She turned to Mark. "My granddaughter's got big plans. *La doctora de la fa- milia.*"

Karen rolled her eyes and drew her grandmother to her side. "Yes, and a little dancing isn't going to change that. C'mon, *Abuelita*, let's dance." Karen walked away with her grandmother. Before she disappeared into the circle of dancers, she turned her head and mouthed "Sorry" to him.

He saluted her and strode to the bar. "Bourbon. Neat," he told the bartender. Yes, that's what he needed: a stiff drink—to match his stiff dick.

Two strong drinks later, the wedding coordinator tapped his shoulder. "Mr. Lansing, we'll start the toasts in a few minutes, okay? We'll begin with Ms. Ramirez and end with you."

He slipped a hand in his pants pocket and pulled out the toast he'd written a week ago. "Yes, that's fine."

The band ended its lively song, and the lights flickered. With a swipe of a towel across his damp face, the lead singer returned to the mic. "Ladies and gentleman, please take your seats."

The guests looked around and then trickled off the dance floor. Karen hugged her grandmother, and then she walked across the room. Her eyes grew wider with each step, and her mouth rounded, as though she were taking and releasing deep breaths.

Mark jumped onto the stage and joined her. She held the mic in a death grip, her knuckles as white as the pristine tablecloths in the room. She glanced at him, but her eyes lacked any focus at all. He tried to give her an encouraging smile, but she looked past him and bit her lip. The chatter eventually died down, and with no speech to fill the void, a smattering of whispered conversations followed.

Still clutching the mic, Karen dropped her head and stared at her shoes.

Something was terribly wrong. A case of stage fright maybe?

Gracie began to rise from her chair, a look of distress on her face.

As discreetly as he could, Mark motioned for her to return to her seat. Then he moved closer to Karen and leaned in. "Can I have the mic?"

She raised her head and blinked several times. Without a word, she let the mic drop into his outstretched hand.

"Sorry, folks. If there's one thing I've learned in life, it's this: Don't tell a woman you'll do one thing and then do the complete opposite. It's a recipe for disaster. You see, I told Karen I'd go first, and then I screwed up by forgetting the order of these festivities. I'm up first, because Gracie and Ethan knew I'd be a pretty easy act to follow."

A few guests laughed, and Karen turned in his direction. "What are you doing?"

He covered the mic with his hand. "Giving you a minute to catch your breath. You need it, right?"

She parted her lips as she nodded her head. God, he wanted to soothe her right then. Wished he could fold her in his arms and tell her everything would be okay. But that would have been far too intimate, and he certainly couldn't do that on a stage at Gracie and Ethan's wedding reception, with her parents and grandmother staring at them expectantly.

Better to lighten the mood and give her time to get herself together.

So that's what he did. And the bride and groom, who'd decided to sit at a table with their parents, smiled throughout his toast, which was gratifying in a way that spoke to how much they'd come to mean to him, not only as individuals but as a couple, too.

And after several minutes, Karen returned to life, smiling along with everyone else. She'd beaten down whatever had spooked her.

When he handed her the mic, she took it without hesitation, meeting his eyes with a clear and steady gaze. He stepped to the side, and she positioned herself in the center of the stage.

"Most of you know Gracie's my sister. But she's much more than that to me. She's my closest friend. My most vocal cheerleader. She's wiped my tears countless times. She did that when I was young, and she did that when I was in college, when the stress and anxiety of taking more courses than I should have became too much. And she's the reason I didn't give up on my dream to go to medical school."

Karen's eyes glistened, and her wistful expression caused a pang in his chest. "We did it, Gracie." Gracie barely held her emotions in check and rose from her seat. She reached the stage and hugged Karen. With their arms around each other's waists, the sisters faced the crowd. Karen lifted the mic to her mouth. "Ethan, make her happy. She deserves it. And since she chose you, I know you deserve it, too. Congratulations to you both." To Gracie, she whispered, "*Te amo.*"

Karen's speech confirmed what he'd already suspected: Her path to medical school hadn't been easy. But she'd done it nonetheless. For someone so young, she had a clear sense of what she wanted to accomplish and an appreciation for the hard work needed to get there. That should have been enough to convince him to get out of her way.

Nope.

He still found himself drawn to her.

Somewhere a Marine was shaking his head in disappointment. So much for the *oorah.*

CHAPTER TEN

Karen sat on a chaise lounge by the hotel's outdoor pool. The faint sounds of the band's drums and brass instruments served as a testament to the fact that the party was still in full swing. She stared at the water, her gaze searching for the source of the occasional ripple that marred the pool's otherwise calm surface. Finally, she glimpsed two sets of iridescent wings. Two dragonflies hovered near each other, until one of them darted away, the other following in its wake.

She knew the moment someone had joined her. As his footsteps drew near, she braced herself for the conversation she didn't want to have.

Mark stood a few feet away, his hands in his pockets and his eyes focused on a cascade of water near the swim-up bar. He didn't turn to her. "Hi."

"Hi."

He gestured to the chaise lounge next to her. "May I join you?"

"Sure."

"Do you want to talk about what happened back there?"

"Not really."

"Okay. Do you want to go skinny-dipping then?"

She laughed. Mark, she'd discovered, had an uncanny ability to either cut straight to the heart of the matter or make you forget the matter altogether—for a few seconds at least. Now, for example, she was picturing him stripping bare and diving into the pool in one fluid movement rather than worrying about the way her nerves had almost ruined her toast.

The planes of his face softened when she sighed. He swung his legs onto the chaise and lounged as though he were spending a care-free day at the beach. "I'm always happy to listen."

That she knew to be true. She'd divulged embarrassing snippets about her sex life to him, and he'd never made a snide comment about them. It didn't appear to be his way. But could she share more? Would he look at her differently then? Maybe. But in her heart, she knew that even if he looked at her differently, he wouldn't think less of her. "Remember when you asked me about medical school the other day?"

He nodded.

"I said I was nervous. And that's true. But it's much more than that. To do well, I need to be able to concentrate on my work. And focus has never been my strong suit."

"Said the woman who got into medical school."

"I never said I can't do it. It just takes a lot of work. Sometimes I don't have enough energy to push myself to get anything done. A task is a task for most people. For me, anything that requires me to focus is a task squared. Or that's at least how it feels, at least."

He furrowed his brow. "Has that always been the case?"

"For as long as I can remember."

He opened his mouth, but that was far as he got before he clamped it shut.

"Go ahead, Mark. I can handle a question or two."

"Did you ever seek guidance about why that might be?"

Oh, God. Why had she decided to go down this road? "My parents took me to a few specialists. I think my mother suspected I had ADD. According to the doctors I saw when I was a teenager, though, I don't. One doctor mentioned hyper-intention."

"What's that?"

"A fancy word some doctor made up to explain away minor problems, I guess."

"I'm sure it's more than that. Tell me."

"It's almost like a self-fulfilling prophesy as I understand it. Like, let's say you're deathly afraid of spiders. You focus so much on that fear that the fear gets worse. In my case, I'm so worried that I won't be able to concentrate in a given situation that I guarantee it."

"Any situation?"

"Highly stressful situations usually. Like meeting new people." She pointed her thumb in the ballroom's direction. "Or being in front of a large group."

"But you've managed it so far."

"Yeah. I'm just worried medical school might be my breaking point. That's one highly stressful situation in and of itself."

"You had to take a big test to get into medical school, right?"

"Yes. The MCAT."

"How'd you get through that?"

"That's just it. I didn't have to. When it comes to my studies, it's never been an issue. It's like my brain is wired to do exactly what it needs to do. It's probably why I'm so focused on my studies. I don't know. When I'm studying, I feel centered. Everything falls into place."

"You're motivated to do great things, Karen. You'll be an excellent medical student and an excellent doctor. You didn't push yourself in college only to stop now."

"You're right. I just wish it didn't have to be this hard."

"Life *is* hard. But all of it doesn't have to be. You're going to stumble, sure, but it's so much easier to get back up when you're stumbling over something that's important to you. Decide what you want to work hard for, and leave the rest of it behind. Focus on what's important to you."

She dropped her head against the back of the chaise and stared at the night sky. "That's your philosophy on life?"

"In a nutshell."

He'd shared his advice as though the solution to her problems was simple. She knew otherwise. And she suspected he did, too; he was a smart guy, after all. One aspect of his statement did pique her interest, however. She turned on her side and propped her elbow against the back of the chaise. "So tell me this. What did you leave behind?"

* * *

His life was not up for discussion, so Mark ignored Karen's question and posed his own. "What time is your flight tomorrow?"

She stretched and rubbed her eyes, reminding him of a sleek feline waking from a restful slumber. "Eleven a.m. Why?"

"Thought I'd give you a ride to the airport, but I'm leaving earlier than that. I could arrange for the car service to pick you up, though."

She yawned. "No, that's okay. Ethan and Gracie took care of everything."

He nodded and checked his watch. "Shall we head back?"

"Mark."

"It's getting late."

"I've shared some very personal stuff with you. So far, you've shared nothing."

"I didn't realize we were keeping score."

"No, we're not. But *friends* share information about themselves."

His gaze traveled over Karen's body. Even at rest, she captivated him.

"What do you want to know?"

"Do you have brothers and sisters?"

"Not really."

"It's a yes or no question, Mark."

"I have a half brother."

She sat up and rubbed her hands together. "*Ooooh.* Now we're getting somewhere." She scooted closer so that their knees almost touched. "Tell me about your parents."

Every muscle in his body tensed, instinct warning him to protect himself from the unpleasant memories ahead. He slowed his breathing, attempting to ease into the conversation as casually as possible. "I grew up with my dad."

She covered his hand with hers. "Did something happen to your mom?"

"Yeah. Boredom."

"Excuse me?"

He'd said too much, but he couldn't figure out how to retract the truth. So he gave her an abbreviated account of his mother's fucked-up departure. "I grew up with my dad. My parents split when I was four or five. My mother was too young. She and my dad had no business getting married when they did, he says. She had big plans, a life to live, a world to see. My dad and I were deadweight. So one day she left. No note, no phone call. Just a voice mail message at my father's work. 'You need to pick up Mark,' she'd said. 'I won't be coming back.'"

He didn't tell her the precise day, but he knew it by heart: September 6. The first day of school. He'd left the house, nerves and excitement warring within his six-year-old belly, and he'd ridden the school bus like a big boy. That afternoon, when he'd jumped off the school bus and barreled through the front door, his father had been waiting for him. His stunned dad delivered the news without preamble. *She's gone*, he'd said. *And she's not coming back.*

Karen moved closer to him. "That's awful."

Her earnest expression worried him. "Don't be so concerned, Karen. I'm not broken because of it. I was too young to know what was happening."

That's what he told himself, at least. He clamped down on his bottom lip, a physical reminder to keep the grittier details to himself. His father's depression. The unkempt house they'd lived in. The way his father's shoulders had slumped every time he looked at his son. Not until he'd been invited to a play date at a friend's house had he remembered people kept tidy homes—and smiled at their children. That was all in the past, though. After a while—several years, in fact—his father had emerged from his funk and learned to be the caregiver Mark needed. And he was grateful for his father's love and support since then.

Karen's gaze bounced around the beach, eventually landing on his face. "But you were a baby. And then your mother was gone."

"I had my dad, and although he didn't know a thing about raising a child, we survived. Together."

"Did you ever reconnect with her?"

"I did. Years later. By then, she and my dad had divorced and she had a new family of her own. I have a brother. A half brother, I mean. She finally settled down after she had him."

"I don't know that I could have a relationship with my mother if she'd left that way."

"It took time, but we're okay now. She calls occasionally, to check on me. Guilt, I guess. And I'm not angry at her. I'm indifferent mostly. She made mistakes. So did my dad."

"Where's your dad now?"

"He lives in Maryland. On Kent Island. I think he's still waiting for my mother to come back to him. He never remarried. Never dated really."

How the hell had they gotten to this point? He never shared anything about his personal life, not voluntarily, and now he'd regurgitated his childhood in the span of minutes. She'd coaxed him into sharing his past with her, and if he didn't guard himself better, she'd take a lot more. He had no inclination to go down the same path his father had stumbled over.

He wanted to fill the silence, but he didn't know what to say. More than anything, he worried about her reaction. And if she pitied him, he had only himself to blame.

She slapped his thigh and smiled. "We're a depressing pair, aren't we? Tell you what. You've been great today. First you got me out of a jam during the reception and then you shared something about yourself even though you had no desire to. For that, I'll let you take me to the casino at the Ritz."

What the hell was she talking about? "Why would I do that?"

"Because the reception is almost over. Because it's our last night in Puerto Rico and I need to live it up for a change. And I'm an excellent blackjack player, so I could teach you a thing or two."

"Blackjack's not my game. Poker's more my speed."

She made a big show of inspecting his face, her eyes bright with amusement. After several seconds ticked by, she widened her eyes. "Oh, you're serious. Mark, I hate to tell you this, but your face doesn't lend itself to poker."

He smiled as he rose from the chaise. "What do you mean by that?"

"It's simple. Your face is a neon sign for your feelings. Mark's happy? The big, open smile appears. Mark's confused? Those eyebrows knit together and you wrinkle your nose."

"I do *not* wrinkle my nose."

"Do, too. Not in the mood to be bothered? The blank stare emerges. And if you're trying to hide your true feelings, you stare at your toes, or your watch, or a spot in the distance."

He caught himself wrinkling his nose and shuddered.

She pointed at him. "See there. You're proving my point."

He reached for her hands and pulled her out of the chaise. "I have an early flight out tomorrow, so I'll have to take a rain check on our casino date."

She pouted. "Fine."

Mark laughed at the disingenuous look of disappointment on her face. He'd spent several minutes in her presence without their mutual attraction stifling them. Had they turned a corner? Maybe the sparks that had flown during their initial meeting had finally been snuffed out.

As they made their way back to the wedding reception, she clung to his arm, cozying up to him in a way she probably thought was friendly, unaware that being this close to her had a dizzying effect on him.

"It's beautiful out here, isn't it?" she asked.

"It is," was all he could manage.

Soft blue and green lights bathed the hotel's grounds, giving the courtyard a majestic appearance. The shadows and dark corners along the hotel's corridors taunted him. He pictured himself maneuvering her into one of those corners and stealing a kiss.

The heat caused him to imagine her wavy hair plastered against her skin, her body languid with lust as he caressed her shoulders, moved his hands down to her waist, and trailed his fingers over her thighs. He squeezed his eyes shut and willed the images to go away.

"You okay?" she asked by his side.

He opened his eyes and gave her a curt nod. "I'm fine."

"You're staring off into space again."

He stopped mid-stride and faced her, a few feet from the garden that fronted the hotel's courtyard. "Drop it, okay?"

Her arm fell away from him. "Okay."

With her eyebrows knitted, she rubbed her upper arms and walked ahead of him. He knew the chill in the air came from his sour attitude, not the temperature.

Dammit. He reached for her, wanting to apologize, needing to explain that his frustration was his problem, not hers. "Karen…"

She didn't slow down and spoke over her shoulder. "Forget about it, Mark. It's okay."

No. It *wasn't* okay, and he could think of only one way to make it right.

So he tugged her to his chest and kissed her.

CHAPTER ELEVEN

*W*ell, that had escalated quickly.

Mark's mouth captured hers. She tasted salt and a hint of sweetness on his lips, a heady combination that made her moan in appreciation. She arched into him, wanting—*no, needing*— to feel his body against hers. He responded by snaking his hand under her hair and caressing her neck. Seconds later, he wrapped his other hand around her middle and stroked her back. Mark's kisses promised a full-body experience, and she shivered in response to all the points of contact. Finally, he drew back, gulping in air. *Oh, right.* She needed to breathe. Funny how easily he made her forget a minor inconvenience like breathing.

She pressed her face against his chest and held on to the lapels of his suit as she took in air. "What's happening?"

He brushed his fingers against her hair. "I'm sorry for acting like an ass."

She looked up at him then. "*That's* your version of an apology?"

He stepped back and ran a hand through his hair. "No, that's my version of being selfish. What I should have done was apologize for being a jerk to you. You didn't deserve it."

She nodded. "You'll get no argument from me there."

He stepped toward her and reached for her hands. "I wanted to kiss you, but I didn't think it would be a smart move, so I took my frustration out on you."

"And the kiss?"

He dropped her hands and shoved his own in his pockets. "The kiss is harder to explain."

"Um, unless I'm missing something, the phenomenon is called attraction. Your pheromones and my pheromones are sending chemo-signals to each other. Totally normal."

He gave her his trademark half smile. "Totally not a good idea, either."

She didn't disagree with him. Doing *anything* with Mark didn't figure in her plans, no matter how much he'd nearly owned her with a single kiss. "Again, you'll get no argument from me. Still, that kiss was pretty freaking hot."

Mark closed his eyes and raised his head to the night sky. "Stop doing that. I'm relying on you to be the voice of reason in this situation."

Ha. That was cute. But she'd oblige him anyway, because she needed to put the kiss in its proper place: a momentary lapse in judgment not to be repeated. If she didn't, he'd consume her thoughts, and she couldn't afford the distraction. "Mark, look around. We're in Puerto Rico. You look hot. I look hot. It's hot, period. And we're standing in front of a garden. You hear that?"

"What?"

"The *coquis*."

"What's a *coqui*?"

She resisted the urge to roll her eyes. "Only one of the most important cultural symbols of Puerto Rico." When he stared at her blankly, she continued. "The tiny frogs, Mark. You must have seen them everywhere at the airport. T-shirts, mugs, hats, you name it. Listen."

They faced each other in silence. "That's their mating call," she told him. "They're practically begging us to lock lips. You can't be faulted for wanting to kiss me under these circumstances."

He bridged the distance between them. "What if I told you I've wanted to kiss you every single second I've been in your presence? Can you explain that?"

She gulped. "Well, that's a little harder to explain."

He pressed his hand against the back of her neck and pulled her flush against him. "And I've never wanted to stop at kissing. I want us to do more than that. *A lot* more."

His breath floated over her face like magic dust, decimating her ability to think clearly. Voodoo. That had to be the reason her logic always failed her when he was near. She simply stared at his lips as he made his case.

"I'll admit this is crazy, and yes, we might regret this, but the attraction I felt for you when we first met isn't going away. I figure we're both adults, and we should be able to see this for what it is."

Yes, yes, yes. Now they were getting somewhere. She nodded in agreement. So enthusiastically she probably looked like a bobblehead.

"Tonight. *Just* tonight. Are we on the same page?"

Karen rubbed two fingers over her lips as she considered his question. For once, she made a conscious effort not to overanalyze the situation. She *wanted* to have sex with Mark. Plain. Simple. And what he'd proposed wouldn't derail her. They'd share a single night together, and no one else would know. If all went well, she'd store enough memories to make her evenings with Sammy Silicone passable—maybe even pleasurable. Brilliant. "Yes, we're on the same page."

He lunged for her then, this time gripping her temples as his mouth descended on hers. Relishing the pressure against the sides of her face, she fisted her hands in his hair with the same intensity. When he trailed his lips over the column of her throat, she dropped her head back. Despite her Mark-induced haze, she registered the sounds of the band grow louder. She turned to see the door of the ballroom closing and sprang away from Mark seconds before two wedding guests stumbled past them.

After expelling a relieved breath, she touched her lips. "Can we get out of here?"

His eyes glossy and half-lidded, Mark responded with a slow nod of his head. That look of arousal made her knees weak and strengthened her resolve.

The night they'd met, she'd opened up to him about her insecurities, and she didn't plan to share them with anyone else. He might claim not to remember what she'd told him, but she knew better. The possibility that she could have a positive sexual experience with someone attuned to her needs outweighed the risks that it would all blow up in their faces. And if she couldn't have great sex with this man, she'd finally have her answer: The problem was her—and always would be.

* * *

Mimi pounced on her the moment Karen entered the ballroom. "Where have you been?"

Shit. Mimi's talent for detecting secrets rivaled her talent for telling inappropriate jokes. Karen relaxed her facial muscles and smoothed her dress. "Oh. Not far. Just outside. I needed some air."

Mimi scanned her face and body as though she were looking for clues to challenge Karen's claim. She opened her mouth and then shut it when her cell phone buzzed. Smiling as she read the message on her phone, she explained, "It's the Marine. His name is Troy."

Saved by a booty call. "Go ahead and answer it."

"He can wait. Listen, I'm meeting him after the reception. I just wanted to let you know, so you're not concerned if I return to the hotel room a little late."

Karen didn't lie often, but when she did, she sandwiched it between two truths. The practice didn't make the lie any less problematic, but it helped her say it without stumbling over her words. "Oh, I hope you have a good time." The truth. "But no need to worry about it. I'm actually going to spend the night with my grandmother." A lie. "I'll make sure to be back here in plenty of time to make our flight." The truth. There. She'd done it.

"Okay. I'll see you in the morning then. Gracie and Ethan are getting ready to leave. I'm going to start making my rounds and saying good-bye."

Mimi left before Karen blurted out the truth: She and Mark would be getting their freak on tonight. The thought gave her pause, so she mentally repeated it. *She and Mark would be getting their freak on tonight.* Her mind struggled to process that fact. To make matters worse, the doors of the ballroom's main entrance opened, and Mark walked in with his cell phone at his ear. Her breath hitched at the sight of him. He'd opened the top two buttons of his shirt, leaving a sliver of his chest exposed. Soon she'd see all of it. Touch it, too.

His steps ate the floor as he made his way to her. Eyes blazing with barely suppressed desire, he advanced with a purpose that made her wonder whether he planned to kiss her in front of everyone. No, he'd never do that. Right?

He stopped a foot away from her. "And you say I have a terrible poker face. You should see your face right now."

No, she was sure she didn't want to do that. She glanced around her to see if anyone was watching them. "Is it really that bad?" she whispered.

"You look like you're having some seriously naughty thoughts."

"Not so naughty, but I'll admit I was thinking about you."

"We'll have to work on that, then. So you can catch up with me."

Gracie came out of nowhere and dropped an arm over Karen's shoulder, pulling them out of the moment. "Careful, Karen. I hear from Ethan that Mark's looking to settle down." Gracie winked at her. "You don't want any part of that, right?"

Karen hid her surprise and smirked, moving her index finger in a circular motion close to her face. "Does this look like the face of someone who wants to settle down?"

Gracie dutifully shook her head. "Certainly not."

"Then Mark has nothing to worry about. But what's this about wanting to settle down?"

Mark furrowed his brow and directed a pointed stare at Gracie. "Not something we need to talk about here. Right, Gracie?"

Jostled from behind by one of her guests, Gracie barely held on to the champagne glass in her hand. Gracie and alcohol never played nicely together. If Gracie had more than one drink in her system, she tended to divulge everyone's secrets. Poor Mark. "Nonsense, *Markito, somos familia aqui*," Gracie continued. When the crease between his brows deepened, Gracie explained herself. "We're family here, Mark. In fact, Karen could help."

Mark, she guessed, hadn't recovered from Gracie's new nickname for him. He mouthed "*Markito*" several times before he shook his head, a dumbfounded expression on his face.

"Anyway, Karen, he's asked us to introduce him to women we think he might get along with. Ethan and I are going to be his dating advisors."

Karen watched Mark fidget under her stare. "Are you now?"

"Not here, though. No point in introducing him to someone who's committed to staying on the island. But once we're back in D.C., I'll be his personal matchmaker. Can't wait, *Markito*."

Gracie trotted off, a swath of silk trailing behind her and a champagne-induced pep infusing her steps.

So he wanted to settle down, huh? How enlightening. Now she knew the reason he'd tried to resist his attraction to her: He was waiting for Mrs. Lansing to walk into his life. Well, his future plans had no bearing on her obviously.

He closed the space between them. "This is awkward."

She tilted her head in feigned surprise. "It doesn't have to be. One night, remember? What you do after that has nothing to do with me."

"Still—"

"Mark, let's just focus on tonight, all right?"

He surveyed her face as though he were counting every single freckle. Apparently satisfied with what he saw, he nodded. "All right."

CHAPTER TWELVE

One minute she and Mark had been waving good-bye to the bride and groom. The next minute he'd whisked her away in a black sedan. With a flick of a button, Mark raised the tinted glass partition, affording them privacy.

After they'd settled themselves inside the spacious backseat, Mark gestured toward the minibar. "Do you want something to drink?"

"No," she croaked. After that, a coughing attack ensued. *Splendid.*

Ever the gentleman, Mark patted her on her back. "You okay? Need me to do the Heimlich?"

She peered at him through narrowed eyes, well aware that his voice shook with laughter. "I'm nervous. I'll be fine." She fanned herself. "Is it hot in here?"

She wasn't fine. Her stomach cramped, nervous energy flowing through her body as she considered what they were about to do. She and Mark were going to have sex tonight. More than anything, she wanted to be in the moment. Whether she could accomplish that was a different issue.

After he poured himself a drink and placed it in the cup holder beside him, he sat back and pinned her with his hooded gaze. "Karen. Don't look away."

His voice soothed her nerves. A little. She gathered enough strength to appear calm and returned his stare.

"Breathe. You're fine."

Speak for yourself, mister.

"Just so you know, I'm a wreck right now."

Well, so much for his confidence. Maybe his poker face was better than she gave him credit for. "Tell me why."

He crossed his arms over his chest and considered her. "I should be clear. I can handle the…mechanics. But I'm nervous about making a mistake. About taking us somewhere we're not supposed to go. Gracie and Ethan…" His voice trailed off.

She understood his point, and they *could* back out now, of course. But what then? She guessed they'd always be on edge with each other, the what-ifs clouding their interactions. Either way, things wouldn't be the same between them ever again. "You know what? We both think too much. Just once, I'd love to be able to do something because it'll feel good. And Gracie and Ethan don't have to know what we do behind closed doors. We're both adults." She scanned his face and torso. "It *is* going to be good, right?"

He laid a hand over his heart, his eyes gleaming. "Your skepticism pains me." His eyes turned smoky then, and he snaked his arm around her shoulder and drew her close. "Let me erase your doubts."

Yes, please. Karen leaned into him, fisting the fabric of his shirt as his lips met hers. Heat. She felt it against her lips. Against her chest. Between her thighs. Even the tips of her ears burned. She un-clenched her fists and trailed her hand down to his erection. When she stroked him, he moaned, the desperate sound echoing her own need.

The sedan slowed to a stop, and they sprang apart. Their heavy breathing filled the silence. She'd been so caught up in him, she hadn't realized they'd arrived at the hotel. The significance of that fact didn't escape her. She wrung her hands and held herself in check when all she really wanted to do was exit the car and sprint to his hotel room.

Mark laid his hand on hers. "Ready?"

Hell, yes, she was more than ready. "Ready."

Mark tapped on the glass partition, and seconds later, the driver opened the back door.

Mark had reserved the Ritz-Carlton Suite, a massive living space on the hotel's ninth floor. Not surprisingly, it rivaled her Georgetown apartment in both size and opulence. Karen's jaw dropped as she toured the suite's interior. It boasted two bedrooms, a living room, a formal dining room, and a professional kitchen. Oh, and one-and-a-half baths. *Of course.* "Must be difficult staying in such a tight space," she told him.

He cocked his head at her and smiled.

The view from the suite's balcony captured her attention. "May I?"

He motioned for her to precede him. "Of course. I'll join you in a minute."

She placed her hands on the wrought-iron railing and raised her face to the evening sky. The mist from the ocean kissed her skin, and the crashing waves lulled her into a languid state. When his footsteps drew near, however, her muscles tightened in anticipation. Then nothing. She turned her head to the side, hoping to see what he was doing without revealing that his presence made her nervous.

"You look beautiful there," he said behind her.

He'd planted himself close enough to breathe into her ear, but far enough that no part of his body touched hers. His failure to bridge that small distance ratcheted up her awareness of it. She heard him shift, and then his lips touched her lobe. "I could stare at you all day."

She tamped down on the urge to squirm from her ticklishness and focused instead on what to say. But she didn't know what to say, not without it rushing out in a jumbled mess, so she settled for a simple *thank you*.

His hands joined hers on the railing, his body caging hers. She fell back against him, reveling in his warmth.

With his lips still pressed against her ear, he dropped his hands and pressed them against the fleshiest area on her hips, kneading her skin with the tips of his fingers. Each caress lifted her skirt higher and higher until he bunched it just above the tops of her thighs. When she moved her butt against his crotch, he dug his fingers into her skin, gripping her hard. That touch, both reverent and desperate, sparked something in her, and her nipples tightened.

She opened one eye, scanning the secluded beach to make sure they weren't being watched. The waves crashed against the shore, matching the tumult within her. He crouched behind her and reached under her skirt, and her eyes fluttered closed. He trailed his fingers up the sides of her bikini bottoms and rested them there. She waited, a tight knot forming in the pit of her stomach.

"I'm trying to figure out what to do here. So many choices. I could rip your panties off. Or I could slide them down your body.

I'd be able to touch your skin as I do it, so it's a slightly better choice. Or I could watch you do it yourself as I stroked my cock."

Karen listened to every word, catching each dip in his voice and noticing the slight change in intonation as his words became more brazen.

He chose to slide her panties down her legs. For a brief moment, she wondered whether he'd noticed that her panties were damp, evidence of how aroused she's become.

"Mark."

He rose and nipped her neck. "Yes?"

"Condom," she blurted out. "Don't forget a condom."

His hands stilled. "Shit. I apologize."

"It's okay, but—"

He stepped back an inch. "Of course."

She turned her head and found him watching her.

"I have to head back inside. But stay there for me. Just like that."

By now he'd bunched her skirt at the waist, leaving the lower half of her body exposed. Could she do it? Remain almost bare and risk someone seeing her?

Before she could answer, he spoke again, his voice low and his words slow. "Spread your legs wider." His voice dropped another decibel. "Please."

Karen gripped the railing and slid her feet farther apart, arching her back so that her butt was on full display. "I think this is what Tyra Banks calls the booty tooch."

He chuckled. "Whatever it's called, I like it. A lot. Be right back. And don't move."

The breeze tickled her exposed skin, and goose bumps dotted her warm flesh.

Karen glanced down her half-naked body. She couldn't have put herself in a more physically vulnerable position, and yet being here with him empowered her, because finally, *finally*, she would focus on her pleasure.

He returned a minute later, his soft footsteps suggesting that he'd removed his shoes. She again twisted her neck to watch his approach. *Oh. My. God.* He hadn't just taken off his shoes, he'd disrobed. Completely.

Wanting to see him in all of his masculine glory, she turned to him. He froze, and she scanned his body, hungry to see every part of him.

"I didn't want you to be the only one exposed," he explained.

His bare chest, with a smattering of hair on it, led to well-defined abs and a deliriously happy trail that pointed to his impressive erection. And his legs? He had impressive muscles there, too. Runner's thighs, she guessed. A hint of a jagged scar on his inner thigh caught her eye, its size unclear from where she stood. She licked her lips in anticipation, wanting more than anything to suck his salty skin, to cause his muscles to contract against her mouth wherever her lips landed. She imagined the tip of her tongue sliding over the ridges of that scar, imagined him fisting her hair the closer she came to taking him in.

For a second she wondered if he'd held off putting the condom on because he didn't want to ruin her first look at his naked body. He didn't strike her as the type to worry about such things, though. Regardless of his reasoning, she appreciated the unobstructed view.

After she'd surveyed him from head to toe, he strolled toward her as though his nakedness were nothing special. But it was. Oh, it was. Caging her against the railing, he leaned into her. Close. But not close enough. "So this is what a beautiful woman with dirty thoughts looks like."

"How can you tell my thoughts are dirty?"

"You're giving me lots of clues. The hungry, glazed look in your eyes. The way you keep pressing the tip of your tongue against your lower lip. Makes me want to smudge that lipstick right off you."

She wanted that, too. So much. Wanted to feel his lips against hers. Hard. Soft. In between. She'd take it all. "Kiss me."

He pressed his body against hers and slipped his fingers through the hair at her temples. She stared up at him. After a brief pause in which she studied the way his eyes went from dark brown to black, their lips met. At first their lips skated over each other, his warm, minty breath mingling with hers. That heat spread through her and emboldened her to deepen the kiss. Her lips felt swollen from the onslaught.

Karen's hands roamed over his body. She massaged his shoulders, relishing the strength under her fingers. Impatient for more, she trailed her fingers up his back and placed her hands at the nape of his neck.

He dipped his head and nuzzled her neck, and she didn't fall into a fit of giggles despite her ticklish tendencies. She considered that progress.

He drew back and rubbed his thumb against her lower lip. "Does the idea of someone watching us turn you on?"

Hmmm. Yeah, it did. In theory. But as soon as he'd planted the thought in her mind, she couldn't stop thinking about all the ways that scenario could end badly for her. Though she knew she should be focused on their lovemaking, she nonetheless played out several versions of that scenario in her head.

She moaned to signal that she was enjoying his thorough exploration of her neck, but in truth she was focused on the scenario in which a group of college frat boys recorded them having sex on the balcony, and then posted the video online. Her grandmother's disapproving face stared back at her. *No. No. No. Don't go there. Please.*

He lowered his hand and dipped his fingers between her thighs, placing two fingers on her clit and rubbing it in a circular motion. "How does that feel?"

Oh, it felt *very good*. But in her head, a police officer with a flashlight shining on her ass, telling them to freeze, appeared.

Mark stilled. Then he drew back and searched her face. "You're in your head, right?"

Would there ever be any hope for her? She buried her face in his chest and murmured her confession. "I can't stop thinking about someone catching us. I'm sorry."

He placed his finger under her chin. "Look at me, Karen."

She looked at him under the veil of her eyelashes.

"Don't be sorry. I'm nothing if not tenacious. We'll adjust."

Her instincts had convinced her that Mark would be patient with her. She was glad to know her instincts hadn't failed her.

"I have an idea." He held out his hand. "Come with me."

Well, yeah. That's what she was trying to do already, wasn't it?

He pinned her with a narrowed gaze and smug grin. "I have to stop saying that to you, don't I? Just take my hand, Karen."

She placed her hand in his and followed him inside. His lazy steps hadn't prepared her for what came next. Suddenly, he used his big body to back her against the wall. So overwhelmed by his abrupt change in tactics, she didn't have the time or the bearings to think about anything but his movements.

"Put your hands on my shoulders."

She did as he asked, and then she rubbed them, because she couldn't resist the opportunity to touch his hard body again. He leaned into her and rolled on the condom he'd been holding in his hand. Then, with a lick of his lips, he lifted her and used his hips to pin her to the wall. She wrapped her legs around him, relishing the warmth of his skin against hers.

"Listen to my voice, Karen."

"I'm listening."

"I want you so goddamn much right now. And if I have to, I'll find the superhuman strength I need to hold you up against this wall until we're both satisfied. Got it?"

She whimpered as she pictured him doing just that. "Got it."

He guided his erection to her entrance and thrust upward.

Karen cried out. "Yes."

He pulled out halfway and swiveled his hips when he plunged back in. "Does it feel good if I rock my hips like this?"

Her mouth couldn't form the words to tell him yes, so she nodded.

He pulled out yet again, a slow and torturous withdrawal that left her breathless for the next time he'd enter her. "And if I slide out slowly, so that you're not sure when I'm going to fill you back up, how does that feel?"

She gave him an honest answer. "It feels so good, it makes my eyes water."

He entered her again, less tender this time, and pumped into her several times in quick succession. "And how does that feel?"

"That's it. Keep doing that. And please don't stop."

He grabbed her ass to get a better hold of her and adjusted her body at an angle. The wall and his thighs kept her upright. "Touch yourself, sweetheart. Make yourself burn even hotter."

She let go of one shoulder, slid her hand down his torso, and placed two fingers on her clit.

Mark groaned and dropped his head into the crook of her neck. "That's so fucking hot."

She hadn't thought it possible, but his cock expanded within her, creating a delicious friction that matched the burn on her swollen clit.

She rubbed and rubbed while he filled her, but somewhere along the way she noticed his arms shook with the exertion of holding her up. As he gritted his teeth and rivulets of sweat trickled down his face, she worried that the orgasm would never materialize. Eventually he'd tire of it all, wouldn't he? And then they'd fall to the ground, a heap of dissatisfaction and exhausted limbs.

He lifted his head from her shoulder and stared into her eyes. "Tell me what you're thinking. And tell me the truth."

"I'm thinking you must be exhausted."

"And you can't relax because you're worried about it?"

"Right."

"I can take care of that."

With one hand, he stripped off the condom and tossed it in the waste bin. Then he hoisted her by her butt to get a better hold of her. Her ass firmly secured in his hands, he strode through the suite. She dropped her forehead onto his shoulder, her mind immediately zoning in on the way his cock pressed against her stomach. She squirmed in his arms, an unfamiliar ache settling in her belly.

When he reached the master bedroom, he set her down in front of him. Unable to anticipate his next move, Karen simply stood there—like an idiot. He cupped her face and leaned over to kiss her. A simple kiss that had a dizzying effect on her.

Still in a daze, she sensed him circle her as though she were his prey. Then he reached for another condom on the nightstand, fell back on the bed, and reclined on his elbows, his gaze trained on her the entire time. What a picture he made. The smattering of hair on his broad chest tapered below his navel, as though it were an arrow pointing to fun times ahead. A few minutes ago, he'd filled her to the hilt. She wanted that sense of fullness again.

Still aroused, he stroked himself as he waited for her to join him. "I'm lying down. I'm comfortable. *Hard* but comfortable. There's no need to worry about me, okay? This is all about you. Now come here and ride me."

Karen climbed over him and moaned when the skin of his thighs touched hers.

"Take my cock in your hands, Karen."

So she did. That alone made him hiss and throw his head back. When she stroked him, the muscles in his neck stretched with tension. "Yes, that's it. Do you feel me getting bigger? Harder."

"Mmmm. Yes. I can't wait to get it inside me, Mark."

Karen realized then that she was writhing on his thighs, the movement stimulating her clitoris with each shift of her lower body.

Mark reached out and cupped her breasts. "You're so fucking beautiful, and your tits are perfect." He pinched each nipple, causing her to cry out and buck against him.

Unable to wait any longer, she grabbed the condom packet and ripped it open with her teeth. After rolling it on him quickly, she centered herself over his cock.

He helped her guide it to her entrance. His eyes never left hers as he teased her, rubbing the tip of his cock against her folds. Karen hovered over him, wanting to engulf him in her wet heat. "Please, Mark. I need you inside me."

He stopped torturing her, finally pushing into her inch by glorious inch. Karen held on to his shoulders and adjusted her legs to take him in as deeply as she could, chanting *yes* over and over. She collapsed over him and threaded her hands through his. And just as he'd asked, she rode him, rising and falling over him in a slow rhythm. When the pressure became too much, she raised her torso and lowered herself on to his cock in shallow bursts.

Somewhere along the way, Mark grabbed her waist, using it as leverage to thrust into her. Together they created the delicious friction that would take them both over the edge.

Karen's eyes widened as the orgasm drew near. "Yes, Mark. Don't stop. Please don't stop."

"I'm on fire, Karen. There's no way I'm stopping."

Her mouth went slack as he increased the tempo of his upward thrusts. Then he switched gears, grinding his torso so that the base of his cock tapped on her clit each time. Several more thrusts later, the orgasm slammed into Karen, making her entire body shake as she rode it out. Then she tightened her vaginal muscles around him, and his strangled moan sent a shiver up her spine.

"That's it, Karen," he said. "That's it." His grip on her waist tightened. "F-u-u-u-c-k," he chanted as his orgasm chased hers.

That could not have been pretty. But it was spectacular. Better than spectacular. And unfortunate, because she wouldn't be experiencing it again, and now she knew what she'd be missing.

* * *

Karen woke to a shrill ring that wouldn't go away. With her head still under the comforter, she extended her arm and patted the nightstand until her hand connected with the telephone. She brought the phone to her ear. "Yes."

"Good morning, Ms. Ramirez."

She sat up, groggy and irritable. "Who is this?"

"This is a courtesy wake-up call, Ms. Ramirez. Mr. Lansing wanted to be sure you didn't miss your flight."

She blinked several times and scanned the master bedroom. Her dress was draped over a chair, and her sandals were neatly tucked under it. "He's gone?"

After a brief pause, the man on the other end of the line confirmed that Mark had in fact departed the island. "Mr. Lansing left for the airport two hours ago. You are free to use the suite until you're ready to go." He cleared his throat. "Will you be needing transport anywhere?"

Yes, she needed to be transported to the land of the thoroughly fucked and discarded. "Um, yes. I'll need a ride to Hotel El Convento. In twenty minutes."

"Very good," the man said. "We'll have a car waiting for you. Have a wonderful day."

"Thank you."

After she'd replaced the receiver, Karen fell back against the mattress. Well, this was a first. She'd often watched a guy scramble out the door after mediocre sex, but no one had ever snuck out on her. Granted, Mark had told her about his early morning flight, but she hadn't expected him to escape before the sun rose.

Sure, the alternative, waking up in each other's arms when they'd agreed to a single night together, would have been awkward. Still, not seeing him at all left her in limbo. Maybe she needed closure. And yes, she needed to know if he'd enjoyed it as much as she had. Given his disappearing act, she suspected the answer was no.

Damn, damn, damn. How could last night have been so one-sided? Yes, the start of their lovemaking had been rocky, but she'd thought they'd glided to the finish line like figure-skating world champions. He'd been attuned to her from the start, giving her the attention and encouragement she'd needed to get out of her head and simply enjoy hot, sweaty sex. *Really hot, sweaty sex.*

All signs suggested that he'd been enjoying himself, too. But maybe he'd been pretending to be as into it as she'd been. Hadn't she pretended to enjoy herself countless times?

Now came the embarrassment. He'd humored her, obviously. And maybe he'd decided not to wake her before he left, so she could suffer through the mortification in private.

She flipped off the covers and sprang out of bed. As she rummaged through the bathroom for a new toothbrush, she silently thanked Mark for a much-needed reminder that her time was best spent on areas of her life where she was likely to succeed, her career being the most important.

This really wasn't a big deal. Karen always prized information, and her experience with Mark revealed two valuable facts: First, she wasn't good in bed. And two, she could live with that knowledge, because discovering otherwise at this point in her life would have been disastrous. She'd spent most of her college years having subpar sex. If she'd met someone who helped her enjoy the moment, and who didn't embarrass her afterward, Karen would have embarked on a sexual awakening that would have impressed even the most jaded porn star. No, this was good news. It reinforced her desire to begin medical school distraction-free.

With a renewed sense of purpose, she readied herself for the drive back to her hotel. On her way out, she reached for her clutch on the kitchen counter and paused when she noticed a single sheet of paper lying next to it. It read:

It's not you, it was definitely them. Thank you for an amazing night.
    —M

She stared at the note and images of their amazing night ran through her brain like a shuffled deck of cards.

It hadn't just been her. He'd enjoyed himself, too. The sex had, in fact, been amazing. She wasn't bad in bed. Damn, damn, damn.

CHAPTER THIRTEEN

Four days after returning from Puerto Rico, Mark stared at the mountain of work that still sat unscaled on his desk. At the moment, he was attempting to review the company's annual reports, but the numbers blurred before his eyes. The buzzing of his office phone cut through the fog.

He hit the speaker button. "Yes, Donna?"

"You have a call from Lisa Heddinger. Would you like to take it?"

He tapped his lips and considered the repercussions if he said no. She'd find a way to get to him eventually—through his father if she had to. It was better for him to bear the brunt of her whims than his dad. "I'll take it." He steeled himself as he waited for the call to be transferred. "Mother. What can I do for you?"

"*Tsk, tsk*, my dear. No need to call me such a horrible name." Her shrill laughter emphasized that she'd been joking. His silence emphasized that he didn't find her funny.

After clearing her throat, she said, "I'm calling for two reasons. First, how are you?"

She never called simply to ask how he was doing. Sure, she asked the question, but the question generally preceded a request of some kind. Today would be no different. "I'm fine. Busy but fine."

"Good. Good. Are you going to ask me how I've been?"

Mark rubbed his temples in a circular motion. "How are you, Lisa?"

"I'm fine, dear. Richard and I divorced six months ago. Irreconcilable differences and all that."

Mark couldn't have been more shocked by the news. Richard had been his father's replacement, the man who'd convinced his mother to settle down and have another child. She'd built a family with Richard and her second son. As a young teenager, Mark had counted the days when that relationship, too, would implode. But that never happened, and eventually Mark accepted the fact that his mother hadn't been averse to commitment; she'd been averse to committing to *them*—his father and him, that is.

As the years passed, though, he'd come to see her in a different light—reluctantly. She'd been young when she married his father. And she'd been unwilling to change her carefree lifestyle to accommodate her family's needs. But he assumed she'd matured over the years, and he couldn't begrudge her efforts to build a different life for herself.

"I'm sorry about Richard." When she didn't respond, he moved the conversation along. "What's the second reason for your call?"

"I'm calling to ask a favor."

Of course she was. "Go on."

"And please hear me out, okay?"

"I will."

"Okay. It's about Spencer."

His half brother, whom he'd never met. "What's the favor?"

"Spencer's accepted a spot at George Washington Law School in the fall. In the meantime, he needs to get his living situation squared away, and I think he needs to get to know the city."

She didn't expect him to babysit his half brother, did she? "What does this have to do with me?"

"He also needs a job."

Hell no. "I can't do that, Lisa. I may be the CEO, but I have a board to answer to. What would he do here anyway?"

"Well, according to your Human Resources Department, the company's looking to hire a legal intern."

It was? In his former role as the company's top financial advisor, he would have known this to be the case, because a legal internship would have involved the use of the company's coffers. But now that he was the CEO, that kind of decision never reached his desk anymore. "You *contacted* the Human Resources Department?"

"Of course not. The department posted an announcement online. I happened to see it."

Not true. As far as he knew, Lisa never *happened* to do anything. Everything occurred by design. Calculation. A little manipulation, even. "Look, Lisa. I appreciate that you contacted me about this, but I have to be honest. Having Spencer here would be awkward."

"He's your *brother*, Mark." Interesting how she wanted him to acknowledge Spencer as his brother when just a few moment ago she'd bristled at being called his mother.

"Let's not push this. Here's what I can do. Send me his résumé. If it looks okay, and I'm assuming it will, I'll send it around to a few of my counterparts in the industry. Someone will offer him a job with my recommendation."

"Wonderful. I suppose that's the best I could hope for."

She paused, and he waited for what always came next.

"How's your father?"

"He's doing great. Can't sit still, so he's teaching a few courses at Chesapeake Community College."

"Good. Good. I'm glad to hear it." She paused again, as was her way. "Is he seeing anyone new?"

The note of uncertainty in her voice shouldn't have touched him—but it did. "He dates but not a lot. That's all I know. We don't talk about dating much. He does his thing. I do mine."

"Are *you* seeing someone new?"

Karen's image appeared in his head. He couldn't call what they'd done dating, but even if they had been dating, his mother lost the right to know the answers to these questions a long time ago. "As I said, I'll check in with Human Resources about the legal intern position. I'll be in touch."

"Always so quick to change the subject. Like father, like son, it seems."

"Didn't have much opportunity to be anything else, did I?"

He refused to be taken in by her soft gasp. Instead of softening his words, he waited.

"Good-bye, dear," she said in a shaky voice. "I'll wait to hear from you."

"Good-bye, Lisa."

Mark tapped the speaker button and swiveled his chair toward the floor-to-ceiling window.

Well, now he felt like a prick. But what did she expect, exactly? That he would pretend she'd always been a part of his life? What a way to start his day. It could only improve from here, right?

Nope. Not right.

That afternoon he participated in a conference call, every second of which tested his patience. At first, he'd wanted to throttle someone. Anyone. But less than ten minutes in, he'd reached the point in the call when he had no more *fucks* to give. The other participants—Ethan among them—argued about the reasons for a delay in the launch of a communications software update.

When he heard the word *shithead* exchanged, he stepped in. "Enough." The ensuing silence told him he had their attention. "This is getting us nowhere, ladies and gentleman. Of course I want to know why the launch will be delayed, but I don't need to know that *now*. If we're working on borrowed time, let's use it wisely. Can someone tell me how we're adjusting the marketing plan to address the delay?"

No one responded.

"Has someone prepared a press release announcing the new launch date?"

Silence. Again.

"Okay. Can someone tell me why the company's launch team appears to be dropping the ball at every turn?"

No one responded to that, either.

"Okay. We'll resume this call when you have answers to my questions. Let me know when you're ready to do that. And If I need to tell HR to start searching for your replacements, let me know that, too."

He disconnected the call and let out a deep sigh. Days like today he yearned for his old job, the one in which he crunched numbers and stared at spreadsheets for twelve hours straight. Really. But as frustrating as that call had been, he knew his agitation stemmed from a more troubling source: The memories of his night with Karen refused to fade.

Fuck.

And he knew exactly how he'd gotten here. Just as he'd predicted, their time together on the island had presented him with one temptation after another, until he could no longer fight the attraction he felt for her. He'd wanted her badly, and he'd lied to himself to justify being with her for one night.

Just one night. To get each other out of their respective systems.

Right.

There'd be no long-term repercussions so long as they both knew the score at the outset.

Right.

With the fires of his attraction stoked, he could turn to the important task of finding a suitable partner.

Yeah. He was beginning to see a theme here.

The moment he closed his eyes, Karen's face appeared; the memory of it, bathed in the moonlight shining through the window of his suite's bedroom, aroused him in seconds each time. He recalled her dazed expression, her flushed skin, and the way her lower lip trembled as she sank down on him. But nothing compared to the memory of the look on her face when the orgasm overtook her: She'd widened her eyes, opened her mouth in astonishment, and let out a soft cry, a mixture of shock and satisfaction that mingled in the air with his own labored breathing. She'd literally taken his breath away, leaving him gasping for air as his own orgasm ripped through him.

Ethan's signature knock startled him out of his daydream. Mark straightened in his chair and ran his fingers through his hair. "Come in."

Now that he was no longer the company's CEO, Ethan had dispensed with wearing suits to work, choosing slacks and dress shirts with rolled-up sleeves as his typical office uniform. His attire wasn't the only thing that had loosened up; Ethan was less stressed these days, too. "Hey. Got a minute?"

Mark waved him in. "Sure. Sit down."

Ethan dropped into the chair. "So I know you were pissed during that call, and you had every right to be."

"I feel a *but* coming on…"

"Well, I'm just checking in, because losing your cool like that isn't like you. It's more like me. The old me, I should say. Is something going on?"

Yes. No. Maybe so. Who the hell knew? He certainly didn't. Ethan's laser-eyed focus on his face made him loosen his tie. "I'm just stressed, Eth. It'll pass."

"You sure?"

"Yeah."

"In that case, man, you know what to do. If you're tense, get laid."

He stared at Ethan. *He'd already taken care of the getting laid part, and now he was tenser than ever.* But he couldn't tell Ethan this. Deflect, deflect, deflect. "I'd be less tense if I weren't so worried about my team's ability to handle the launch."

Ethan grimaced and stood. "Mistakes were made. Not by me. You'll see that soon enough. But in the meantime I'm on it. I've got your back, buddy."

"That's what I need to hear."

Ethan angled his head and considered him. "You know…"

"Say it, Ethan."

"I was just thinking about the Masters Tech Gala. You're going, right?"

Sponsored by Visnet Technologies, the Masters of Technology Gala celebrated the region's technology professionals and forward-thinking companies. His secretary had placed it on his calendar, and he'd promptly forgotten about it. Until now. "Of course I'm going. It's part of the job description. You?"

Ethan shook his head and smiled. "No way. Not part of the job description anymore."

"Lucky you."

"Anyway, I was just thinking you could take a date to the gala. I don't know, maybe call Sharon Castellano and invite her to join you."

Mark kept his face blank. As soon as she and Ethan had returned from their abbreviated honeymoon, Gracie had contacted him, singing the praises of a former graduate school classmate. Sharon, according to Gracie, was whip smart, confident, and successful. But none of that changed the fact that he didn't want to call her. Not after he and Karen had spent a night together. *Too soon*, he'd argued to himself. Eventually, he'd call Sharon, but not yet.

"It'll give you a chance to see how she handles the networking and social demands of being with someone like you. Some people aren't cut out for that shit."

"I'm not going to *test* the woman, Ethan."

"I didn't say you had to *test* her, Mark. This is all about compatibility, is all I'm saying."

"I'll think about it."

"Don't think about it too long. The gala's only a week away."

"Got it, Mommy."

Ethan gave him the finger. "You asked for my help. Don't be an asshole when I give it to you."

"Sorry, man. You're right. You might not believe this right now, but I really do appreciate your help. "

Ethan gave him a carefree smile. "Hey, it's the least I could do. You dropped everything to attend our wedding. It meant a lot to us."

"I'm glad I went. I had a great time."

"All that was missing was a hot woman to keep you company." Ethan lifted a brow and gave him a cheesy smile. "That would have made the trip even better, right?"

A hot woman had kept him company. And yes, her company made the trip even better. But his plan to have a one-night fling had backfired. He wanted to see her again. Which made the situation worse. *Much worse.*

Before he left, Ethan snuck in one last reminder. "Don't forget my suggestion about inviting Sharon to the gala. You have to start somewhere."

And that was the problem, of course. He couldn't muster enough interest to pick up the phone and call the woman. Not when he couldn't get Karen out of his head.

One night.

Right.

CHAPTER FOURTEEN

Exhausted from a four-hour medical school orientation, Karen came home, used the bathroom, and dove under the covers. Nothing—and she truly meant *nothing*—would get her out of the bed for the rest of the evening.

She considered the orientation a resounding success. For one thing, she'd been able to focus on the presentations, taking notes on the professors' expectations of their students and the options for her spring clinical schedule. In less than six months, the medical school would unleash her and her classmates on an unsuspecting public; they'd have the opportunity to assist with taking patient histories and shadowing more experienced medical students and doctors. The orientation had covered the do's and don'ts of interacting with patients.

For another thing, she hadn't thought about Mark once—and given how often she'd thought about him the past week, that was a significant feat. But now she lay in bed and memories of her night with Mark returned in full force. She closed her eyes, and a vivid image of Mark staring up at her under the veil of his thick eyelashes came to her.

Her night with Mark had changed her in ways she'd never anticipated. Now she knew the sensation of being stretched to capacity. Now she knew a man could dig his fingers into her hips as she rode him and the bite of pain would make her tighten around him. Now she knew that she could make a man come hard simply by telling him how he made her feel. Moaning from the memories alone, she slid her hand under the comforter, trailed her fingers down her stomach, and imagined Mark's soft lips marking her body as his.

Her cell phone rang, and she blindly reached for it. *What a stupid move.* Her hand accidentally tipped the phone off the nightstand, and the phone clattered to the floor. Stretching her torso over the edge of the mattress, she scooped it up. Though she tried to clear her voice of any signs of her arousal, her greeting still came out breathy. "Hello?"

"Karen."

If she'd had her hand on her clit right then, Mark's rough voice would have taken her over the edge. She blew out a slow breath. *Keep your cool, chica. No fawning over a man allowed.* "Mark, this is a surprise."

"How have you been?"

He'd called to shoot the breeze? How odd. "I'm fine. You?"

"I'm fine, too."

Except he didn't sound fine. His voice held none of the playfulness she'd come to associate with him. Instead, she got the distinct impression he resented the need to contact her. "What's up, Mark?"

"I have a favor to ask of you."

Never in a million years would she have expected Mark to call and ask her for a favor. Not after they'd agreed to go their separate ways. Not after he'd left Puerto Rico without saying good-bye. She understood why he'd done it—or she thought she did, at least. What they'd done on the island was an interlude to be tucked away, never to be discussed again. Despite her acknowledgment of these facts, she couldn't shut off her feelings at will. Even now, their tenuous relationship was in its raw phase—the phase in which simply seeing him would make her nervous and edgy. Anything he asked of her would be overshadowed by that fact. "What do you need?"

"I'm attending a gala next week, a sort of who's who of the technology industry, and I need a date. I was hoping you'd join me. As my friend, of course. But I'd understand if you didn't want to go. I just figured you might enjoy yourself, and it would make the evening bearable for me."

For a moment, she wondered if she'd hallucinated the whole exchange. He wanted to take her to a black-tie affair? As friends? Yes, she envisioned them being in the same room together a few months from now. But being together one-on-one, next week, at an event where presumably they'd be expected to dance, too? If she had masochistic tendencies, sure that would be fine. But she didn't. She swallowed in an unsuccessful attempt to moisten her dry throat. "I don't—"

"I want to see you," he said.

A flutter skipped across her belly at his words. *Oh, she hadn't seen that one coming.* Her gaze darted around the room in search of an object to focus on. Without an anchor for her thoughts, she wouldn't be able to finish the conversation. She settled on the stethoscope her parents had given her as a graduation gift. "Is that the real reason you called?"

She held her breath as she waited for his answer. Seconds ticked by. Was he still there? "Mark?"

"I'm in a hotel room in Miami, thinking about you. I called because I had to. I—"

She held her breath as the silence stretched beyond a few seconds, not knowing what to expect. Her death grip on her cell phone cramped her fingers.

"I want to see you," he added.

His confession emboldened her. If he could admit it, so could she. "I'd like to see you, too."

"Okay, we've established that we want to see each other again." The lightness in his voice had returned. "So what do we do about it?"

"Not sure."

"Well, since we're being so open with each other, I have another confession to make."

She'd reached her quota for confessions in a single night. Any more and she'd be a wreck. Oh, who was she kidding? She was already a wreck. "Lay it on me, Lansing."

"I wish I could reach through this phone and touch you."

"And I have a confession."

"Tell me." His voice had lowered to a whisper.

"I wish you could reach through this phone and touch me, too."

"Are you in bed?"

"I am."

"So am I."

Phone sex was virgin territory to her, but she very much wanted to change that. It would serve as a bridge between their last sexual encounter and their next one—because unless she was seriously misinterpreting this conversation, there would *definitely* be a next one. "Are you naked?"

He chuckled. "No, but I can fix that."

"So can I. Ready. Set. Go."

She dropped the phone on the mattress, threw her tank top over her head, and slipped off her panties. Gah. The stethoscope. She couldn't look at it without thinking of her parents, so it definitely had to go. She ran to the other side of the room, grabbed the stethoscope, and placed it outside her bedroom door. *So* much better.

She dove under the sheets. Next, she moved to pick up the phone and stopped herself. Staring at the palms of her hands, she debated whether to pick up the phone with a tissue, until an idea came to her: speakerphone. Brilliant. She gingerly pulled a tissue from the box and depressed the speaker button. "Mark? You still there?"

"Yeah. I'm done, though."

"What?" She winced at the panic in her voice. "Did you—"

"I'm kidding. Got everything you need. Candles? Soft lighting? Music?"

"Ha, ha. Bear in mind I could do this without you, Lansing. I've had *lots* of practice."

His groan echoed in her room. "Now I'm really done."

She laughed. Silence followed. And for once she welcomed it.

"Close your eyes, Karen. Focus on my voice."

She complied without hesitation. "I'm listening."

"I want you to use your imagination. If I were there, this is what I'd do to you. I'll guide you. Is that okay?"

She rubbed her thighs together, the pressure between her legs already building. "Yes," she managed to say.

"Good. If I were there, I'd use the tips of my fingers to caress your jawline. I'd kiss your jawline, too. Then I'd trail my index finger down the center of your neck. You with me?"

She mimicked his words, imagining her hands were his, each movement a featherlight touch against her heated skin.

"I'd move down to your breasts. I wouldn't be able to stop myself from placing my big hands on your beautiful tits. I'd massage them. Would you like that?"

Karen placed her hands on her breasts and kneaded them. Her nipples tightened at the contact. "Yes. I'd love that, Mark."

"Now imagine me sucking your nipples. They'd tighten into stiff peaks. You'd be so turned on that you'd reach for my cock. Would you stroke it for me, Karen?"

"Oh, God. Yes, I'd stroke it. It's so thick. My fingers wouldn't be able to close around it completely."

"Ah, Karen," he hissed. "My dick is so fucking hard right now just thinking about it."

Her fingers froze on her chest as his words worked their way to her core. She squeezed her muscles, wanting to draw out her arousal, and they pulsed in response. She flexed her feet to release the tension from curling her toes into the mattress. "What now?"

"I'd ask you to spread your legs, and then I'd settle my upper body between them. I'd spend some time looking at you. You'd be wet, wouldn't you, Karen?"

Oh, he knew how to torture her. "Yes, Mark. I'd be so wet for you. I'd be glistening. And I'd use my fingers to spread my lips, so you could see how wet you've made me."

He moaned.

At this point she couldn't stop herself from writhing against the mattress. She imagined his dark eyes watching her as she opened herself to him. "Are you touching yourself, too?"

"I am. My hand is wrapped around my cock. Right now I'm going slowly. I'll pick up the pace soon."

Her mouth fell open at the thought of him naked in his bed and stroking himself.

"Now back to you," he continued. "Slide your hands down your stomach. Now give your hips a gentle squeeze. Your fingers are small compared to mine, but just imagine my fingers gripping your hips. Imagine the pads of my thumbs resting on your skin, pressing against your hips and kneading them. Still with me?"

If she were any more with him, she'd teleport herself to his hotel room. "Oh, yeah. I'm with you."

"Place your fingers outside your pussy, baby. Massage your lips. Now open those folds. Feel the air touch that wet flesh. It's wet, right?"

She tapped her clit and confirmed that she was soaked. "Yes, I'm wet."

"Okay. Take some of that wetness and spread it around. Now that you're ready, rub your clit. Slow circles only."

She circled her clit with her fingers, but it wasn't enough. "Can I go faster?"

"No. Slow. Tell me how it feels."

"I feel so much heat between my legs. And my muscles are tense. My clit is throbbing. And if I squeeze, it throbs even harder."

"Jesus. I'm picking up the pace, Karen."

"I need to rub it faster."

"Yes, rub yourself faster, harder. Make yourself feel good."

She rubbed her clit in hard circles. Over and over. Again and again. Until her back arched off the bed. She rose on an elbow and looked down at herself. "I'm imagining your head between my legs, licking me, sucking me. I'm going to come soon."

"So am I, baby. And I wish with every fiber of my being that I could finish you off."

She closed her eyes and moaned. "I'm close, Mark." A few circles more and her body tightened almost painfully as the orgasm hit her. "Oh, God. That's it. That's it. Yes. Yes."

His moans grew louder as hers softened. "Karen, I'm coming too," he said, his voice tight and gritty.

She emerged from the haze and listened to the sounds of his heavy breathing. He'd done it again. Made her forget everything but him and the feelings he'd managed to draw out of her. Sated, she turned on her side and stretched. "That was incredible." She finished the declaration with a huge yawn.

"Indeed it was."

"I'm so glad you called."

"Which reminds me. Will you come to the gala with me?"

Oh, right. She'd forgotten the reason for his call. In her muddled state, she blurted out her question. "As your friend?"

The ensuing silence warned her she wouldn't like his answer.

CHAPTER FIFTEEN

Karen's question hit him like a sucker punch to the gut. It was a fair question, but he didn't know how to respond to it.

He needed more time to come up with a coherent answer. "Give me a sec." He sprang from the bed and toweled himself off. Deciding to go commando, he slipped into his jeans.

He picked up the phone again and paced the room. "I have a feeling this is a trick question. I'm screwed either way, right?"

She laughed. "No, I just want to know what you're thinking. Just so there's no confusion."

"Karen, I assure you, there's confusion."

She snorted on the other end of the line, and he smiled. "I'll give you ten points for honesty, Lansing. And I'll put you out of your misery. Tell me about this tech gala."

"It's a black-tie affair. Lots of schmoozing. Decent food. Plenty of quality liquor to get us through the worst of it."

"As you know, I'm not much of a drinker."

"Dancing. There'll be dancing. I might even be able to get the band to play a salsa song, so we can put our new moves to good use."

She sighed. "I'd like to go with you. It's just…it's the kind of event that would make me nervous, and you know what happens when I'm nervous. You'll have a babbling idiot for a date…"

The tension left his body, and he grinned. "We make a good team, remember? If you start babbling, I'll cover for you."

The sound of her clucking her tongue meant she was at least considering it, right? "I don't know, Mark. Wouldn't you prefer to go with someone who'll make you look good?"

"I want to go with you. So before you stomp all over my heart, let's discuss the basics. Do you have something to wear? It's a black-tie affair."

"I could borrow something from Mimi. She's about my size, and I know she attends these kinds of events for work all the time."

"Okay. What about your availability. It's next Saturday at seven."

"My social calendar is decidedly antisocial these days, so that's not an issue."

If he asked her about her social calendar, they'd get sidetracked. But eventually he'd ask her about her friends. So far she hadn't mentioned any. "Okay. You have access to a dress. You're available. And you'll get to spend the evening with me."

"At a tech gala where a bunch of techies will talk tech. You'll have to forgive me for not signing up this minute."

"I'll take you home with me and thank you for your time."

She whistled. "Breaking out the big guns, huh?"

"One gun in particular."

"*So subtle*. When will you pick me up?"

"Six thirty. Bring an overnight bag. I'd like you to stay the night. We'll talk then." The words tumbled out before his brain could catch up and retract them. He could pretend his dick was running the show, but he knew his dick had no interest in sleepovers. Which meant what, exactly? Fuck it. He didn't care to examine his motivations any further. "So yeah, I have to go, but I'm looking forward to Saturday. Good night, Karen."

"Good night, Mark. Thanks for calling. I know I gave you a hard time, but I'm really glad you called."

He swore he could hear the smile in her voice; it reached through the phone and brightened his dark hotel room. Yeah. He was in trouble.

* * *

Karen turned sideways and inspected her reflection in the mirror as she debated whether to wear Spanx. She took a deep breath and sucked in her stomach for as long as she could, blowing out air only after she risked turning blue. Spanx would have been nice, but if she and Mark had sex that evening, the process of getting the contraption off her would turn into a tug of war. Plus, she wasn't feeling well—nervousness, she supposed—and being squeezed to death by a spandex boa constrictor wouldn't help matters. No Spanx.

Mimi had come through for her with a stunning dress. The steel blue one-shoulder gown hugged Karen's curves and gave the illusion that her breasts defied gravity. It featured a cowl back with a clever strip of trim that allowed her to wear a bra without disturbing the open-backed design. A silver clutch and silver peep toe shoes completed the ensemble.

The buzzer for her apartment sounded. She pressed the intercom button. "Yes?"

"Karen, it's Mark."

"Hi, Mark. Come on up."

After she buzzed him in, Karen fussed with her hair one more time. Her thick locks would never hold a chignon without numerous cans of hairspray, so she'd left her hair loose, a single crystal clip holding it back on one side.

Mark rang the doorbell, and she opened the door. They stared at each other, and she held on to the door for support as she got her first look at him. He'd gone for a classic black tuxedo and bow tie, and the jacket fit his broad shoulders perfectly. The rich fabric of the tux contrasted with the delicate silk on the lapels. He'd draped a silver silk scarf around his neck, which begged for her to take its ends and tug him to her. So she did. "You look handsome."

His eyes, dark and assessing, softened. "I'm not sure any words could describe how incredible you look. I want to kiss you so badly right now."

"Let's take this inside, then," she said as she pulled him into the apartment.

As soon as she closed the door, he whipped her around and pressed her against it. His lips swept over hers, seeking entrance, and when she parted her lips, he licked his way inside her mouth. The taste of him, a hint of coffee chased away by peppermint, intoxicated her. She cradled his jaw with her hands and melded her body to his, wanting to get as close as she could to him.

He broke away and lowered his mouth over her bare shoulder. Her legs wobbled like they were made of gelatin, so she grabbed on to his waist for support.

"We have to go," he murmured against her shoulder.

"Yes, I know."

"Do you have a bag ready?"

She pointed to her bag, which she'd set on the floor by the couch. "My walk-of-shame rescue pack is ready to go."

He picked the bag up and held her hand. "Let's go then. I want to be sure you get to use it."

* * *

Karen couldn't contain her awe as she walked up the stairs of the Andrew Mellon Auditorium. With its limestone façade and terra-cotta-tiled roof, it resembled a museum—or a place where people conducted important business—and it intimidated the hell out of her. Inside, however, the event organizers had transformed the austere space, projecting a starry night sky onto the walls and vaulted ceiling, and filling the space with flowers and greenery.

Mark held her hand and led her to the outer edge of the massive room. She didn't know anyone here except Mark and that fact alone made her nervous. "How long do we have to stay?"

He threaded his fingers through hers and squeezed her hand. That squeeze comforted her in a way that his words couldn't. It said he was there for her. "I'll make the rounds. Then we'll have dinner, listen to the awards, and leave."

She stared up at him. "Were you *trying* to be helpful? That sounds like the whole night to me."

He grinned and tugged her toward the center of the room. "You'll be fine."

A mountain of a man in a midnight blue tuxedo slapped Mark on his back. "How are you, Mark?"

"Just fine, Baxter."

Mark pulled her against him. "This is Karen Ramirez. A friend of mine."

Baxter gave her a friendly smile. "A pleasure to meet you, Karen. You look lovely tonight."

Karen shook off her shyness and returned his open smile. "A pleasure to meet you, too. How do you know Mark?"

"Mark and I worked together, before he jumped ship with Ethan. It was a smart move. I left the company six months later."

Mark covered his mouth and leaned toward Karen, pretending to whisper. "Don't let the muscles fool you. The guy's brilliant. But don't tell him I said that. His head's too big already."

Karen relaxed once she realized neither man took himself too seriously.

"Congrats on the award, Bax," Mark said.

Baxter looked down at his toes. "Thanks."

Karen marveled at the fact that this big, beautiful man shied away from the attention. "What kind of award are you getting?"

Baxter's face lit up. "The Vanguard in Education Award."

"Baxter designed a program for online education that will allow grade schools in the same district to plan and conduct virtual classes together," Mark explained.

Baxter chimed in. "It's not the first of its kind, but I've tweaked the software to make the chat rooms and messaging functions user-friendly for kids in grade school."

"I've seen a demo, and it's impressive," Mark told her.

Karen couldn't help noticing the pride in Mark's voice. "How is it different from other virtual-learning systems?"

Both men's eyes widened, and she laughed. "I'm a recent college graduate, gentlemen. A quarter of my classwork in my senior year happened online."

Baxter jumped into a detailed description of the program—perhaps *too* detailed—until a woman joined them and disrupted Baxter's flow.

"Well, well. If it isn't tall, dark, and disinterested in the flesh," the woman said to Mark.

Karen glanced at him, expecting to see annoyance flash across his face, but his eyes shone with merriment instead.

"Hello, Symone," Mark said.

Karen gawked at the woman who returned Mark's stare with a wry grin. Sun-kissed corkscrew curls surrounded an arresting face dominated by high cheekbones and full lips. Her light brown eyes promised that she would be fun to hang around with, no matter how regal her physical appearance. And her tangerine gown complemented her brown skin, ensuring that she'd never fade into the background in the sea of black attire at the gala. Karen was smitten. It was official: she'd now experienced her first girl crush.

Mark shifted to allow Symone into the circle. "Symone, this is Karen Ramirez. A friend of mine. Karen, this is Symone Powell. A friend and colleague. Symone, you remember Baxter, right?"

Mark's voice held a hint of amusement. To Karen's surprise, Baxter clenched his jaw, barely suppressed annoyance etched into his face. If Symone noticed his disapproval, she didn't let on.

Symone smiled at Karen. "It's lovely to meet you."

"Likewise."

Symone used her index finger to inspect Karen's bracelet. "That's beautiful."

Karen hadn't expected a compliment. "Thank you. It was a gift from my sister."

Symone angled her head and assessed her. Her gaze traveled over her face, darted to Mark's, and settled again on Karen. "You're beautiful, dear. And young."

In that instant, the tone of the encounter threatened to change. Karen braced herself for an insulting remark, the champagne roiling in her stomach and making her queasy.

"I didn't realize Mark and I have that in common—an appreciation for young and beautiful people, that is."

Mark laughed. "You've elevated it to an art form, Symone."

Karen expected that Symone would make a stinging remark at her expense, but she needn't have worried. Symone meant to tease, and Mark was her target.

Symone smirked, and she and Mark exchanged playful looks.

"It'll be her downfall, too," Baxter added.

Symone's nostrils flared, but she held her tongue. The tension between Symone and Baxter blanketed the small space. Mark must have picked up on it, too, because he moved closer to Karen and gave her hand another squeeze.

A handsome young man strode toward them with two champagne flutes in hand. His dark brown skin gleamed, its smoothness the perfect setting for his strong facial features.

Symone followed his approach. "Ah. There's one of the young and beautiful people now. He's blessed with plenty of stamina, too."

Baxter cleared his throat. "Karen, would you like to join me on the dance floor?"

She glanced at Mark, whose gaze focused on a point beyond Baxter's shoulder. "Sure. I'd love to."

Baxter placed his hand at the small of her back and ushered her away. Issues. These people had issues.

* * *

Symone pinned him with an assessing gaze. "She's lovely, Mark."

Mark watched Baxter and Karen on the dance floor. "She is." Baxter spoke into Karen's ear, and she laughed. It didn't worry him, though, because he knew Baxter's only weakness was the woman standing next to him.

Symone raised her champagne glass to the air and inspected its color. "Is she temporary?"

Mark hated the question. It cheapened what he and Karen shared despite the incontrovertible fact that the honest answer was yes. So he dodged the question altogether. "It's nothing like that."

Symone turned to her companion, who seemed content to do nothing more than serve her needs. "Bryce, I'd prefer wine. Could you get me a glass of Merlot instead?"

Bryce bowed. Yes, he actually bowed as though Symone were his queen. "Of course. I'll be right back."

With Bryce out of earshot, he turned to Symone. "Is he in training?"

Symone grinned. "He is. And coming along nicely, I might add."

He'd known Symone several years. When he'd served as the company's top financial advisor, Symone had been his counterpart at a technology company in Alexandria. They'd become fast friends after attending an executive retreat two years ago. Much to his regret, he'd introduced her to Baxter before he realized Symone had no use for men with their own opinions.

"Do you think you'll ever tire of these temporary liaisons?"

"Eventually, sure. But for now I'm doing their future wives a favor. I have my say. They obey. We play, and then I send them on their way."

"Spoken like a true Kanye West wannabe."

Symone burst out laughing and pushed his shoulder. "You're such an ass."

"And you love me for it."

She returned her attention to Karen and Baxter as they continued to dance. A line appeared between Symone's brows. Mark suspected it was prompted by Baxter's presence, not Karen's. "It's okay to not be serious about someone, Mark. Just don't send mixed signals. That's how people get hurt. You don't want to hurt her, do you?"

Mark shoved his hands in his pockets. "I've got it under control, Symone."

Just then, Karen's gaze met his, and she smiled. He lifted his champagne glass to his lips, doing his best to ignore the slight tremble in his hands. Well, maybe he didn't have it under control. But he planned to fix that soon.

CHAPTER SIXTEEN

Karen glanced at Mark as he drove. "Okay, so are we going to talk about it?" She continued to rummage through her overnight bag searching for her flats. *Cinderella would have had it so much easier if she'd have thought to bring a walk-of-shame rescue pack to the ball.*

Mark drummed his fingers on the steering wheel and kept his eyes on the road. "Talk about us?"

"Yes. Us. What we're doing. Again, just so there's no confusion. And this time I won't be giving you a pass."

He took a deep breath and blew it out slowly. "Fine. I'm just going to put this out there. I like you, Karen. A lot. But I know you're starting medical school soon, and you've made clear that you're not looking to attach yourself to anyone."

"Exactly. And you're looking for a wife."

He groaned. "I'm *not* looking for a wife. I'm looking to *date* someone."

"You're looking for a committed relationship then."

"Eventually, yes."

"I'm curious. You asked for Gracie and Ethan's help finding some-one to date. Why? I mean, I can't imagine there's a shortage of women interested in dating you."

"Finding someone to date isn't the problem. It's the actual dating that's going to be a challenge. Old habits die hard. And my habits are of the 'that-was-great-maybe-we'll-do-it-again-sometime' variety. "

"Ugh. I'm not sure I wanted to hear that."

"You asked for honesty, remember?"

She rolled her eyes. "I'm so naïve. Not sure what I was thinking when I asked for you to be straight with me. Go ahead and feel free to lie just a bit." Mark's take on dating fascinated her. She adjusted herself in the passenger seat so she could look at him. "Now I'm su-per curious. Did you give them a wish list?"

He scoffed at the question. "A wish list? No. I'm not looking to date a product on Amazon."

"C'mon. Let's be real. If you talked to Ethan about this, there was definitely some objectifying going on."

"We just discussed certain attributes that might be ideal."

"I knew it," she said as she slapped his lap.

"Careful. You might hurt yourself."

He might not want to talk about it, but she certainly did. Which meant she wasn't going to let up until she got an answer. "Okay, out with it. What were these attributes?"

"I can't remember them off the top of my head."

She narrowed her eyes and stared at him.

After several seconds of silence, he relented. "Okay, okay. Some-one around my age. Established in her career. Someone who's fig-ured out where she wants to live, whether she wants kids. You know, the big stuff."

In other words, she and the future Mrs. Lansing had nothing in common. Her throat tightened at the realization that she'd never be a serious prospect for him. Why it mattered, she didn't know. "What about in the looks department?"

"Oh no, we're not going there."

"All right, all right. You've been remarkably candid with me. I appreciate that. But now I'm very confused."

"How so?"

"Well, if you're on the hunt for Mrs. Lansing, why are you taking me to your place?"

* * *

This time Mark had an answer. "Because I think we both could use a last hurrah."

"A what?"

"A last hurrah? A fling. And before you shut me down, hear me out."

"I'm going to regret this, I'm sure."

She sat next to him, wide-eyed and curious, with more cynicism in her body than any twenty-two-year-old should possess, and he couldn't help smiling. "No editorial comments, please."

She rolled her eyes and gestured at her lips as though she were zipping them shut. "The floor is yours."

He eased his car into his designated space in the lot behind his condo. "Let's take this discussion inside, all right?"

"All right," she said as she grabbed her overnight bag.

He took her bag and led her along the path that would take them through the building's gated courtyard.

"Mark, this is gorgeous," she said behind him.

"Different, right? This building once served as an embassy. It was converted into this condo a decade ago. Five floors and six units. I have the top unit."

"You're so modest. The penthouse, you mean?"

"Yes, the penthouse, if you can call the sixth floor of a building a penthouse. It's one of the few true loft spaces in Washington, D.C., I fell in love with it when I saw it."

"Can't wait to see what a true bachelor pad looks like."

"What exactly are you expecting, Ms. Ramirez?"

She stepped into the elevator. "Leather. Lots and lots of leather. Oh, and black satin sheets." With laughter in her eyes, she continued, "Maybe even a disco ball or two."

He inserted the card key and pressed the button for the penthouse unit. "No, no, and *hell* no."

"A swing?"

"Definitely not."

"You're a disappointment, Mark."

She said this with a pout, her pretty lips begging to be kissed. This woman got to him in ways he'd never expected. It was always the little things. The flash of vulnerability behind the bravado. A hitch of her breath. A smirk. And now a playful pout. He dropped her bag on the elevator floor and used his body to push her against the wall. "I can fix that, I promise."

She reached out and hung on to his lapels, drawing his upper body closer to hers. "This makes no sense," she whispered.

Mark didn't disagree, but what he had in mind didn't require them to make sense. He swept his lips across her forehead. "Sometimes the things that bring you the most pleasure make no sense."

She buried her face in his neck and tightened her hold on the lapels of his jacket. "Well, let's be seriously idiotic, then."

The ding of the elevator surprised them both, and they broke apart. As they entered the loft, Mark tried to picture his place through Karen's eyes. He'd never been nervous about bringing a woman to his home—until now. Which made one fact clear: Her opinion mattered to him.

She stood in the middle of the room and spun to give herself a panoramic view of the open space. "*Very* nice. I like splashes of color, so it's a little austere for my taste. But it's a perfect space for a single man. Speaking of which, where are the dirty gym socks?"

He laughed as he removed his tuxedo jacket. "In the hamper, where they should be."

"No separate office space, though."

"That's the idea. I hate to bring work home with me. If there's no office, I won't be tempted to work here."

She gave him a nod of approval. "Makes sense. And I like it. Tastefully decorated. Clean. What more could a booty call ask for?"

Though her eyes shone with laughter, her tone bore an edge he'd never heard before. He didn't like it. "Karen, you're not a booty call."

She cleared her throat and looked down at her shoes. "I'm not? Then what am I?"

He closed the distance between them. "You're a woman who's attracted to me. I'm a man who's attracted to you. We're both about to experience big changes in our lives. You're off to medical school. I'm trying to curb my bachelor ways. Let's think of this as our last fling."

"Until I head off to medical school?"

"Yes."

"That's in three weeks."

He nodded. "Let me show you a good time for those three weeks. You'll go off to medical school with no distractions and pleasant memories. Don't you owe it to yourself to have a little fun before you focus on your studies?"

With her head angled in contemplation, she bit her lip and studied him. "In case you haven't noticed, fun isn't a high priority for me."

"What about sex? Is sex a high priority for you? Because that's part of the package, too."

CHAPTER SEVENTEEN

The man excelled at saying exactly what she needed to hear. As soon as he'd said sex was part of the package, too, her lady bits perked up, eager to join the conversation. "That's quite a package."

He swept his arm in the air like a game show host. "And it could all be yours for the low, low price of spending time with me."

She cracked a smile, no longer able to pretend she wasn't taken in by his playfulness. "You drive a hard bargain, Mr. Lansing, but with perks like that, there's no way I can refuse. So when does the fun begin?"

His eyes turned smoky, and he stared at her under the veil of his long eyelashes. "First, we should seal the deal with a kiss."

That was just fine with her, so she sauntered toward him, her anticipation building with each step. When she reached him, he slipped his hands under the curtain of her hair and tugged her close. Karen closed her eyes and lost herself in the kiss. His mouth mastered hers, and she followed its commands.

All too soon, he pulled back. "That was nice, but that wasn't the kind of kiss I was talking about." Without further explanation, he dropped to his knees and reached under her dress. "What's it going to take to make you wet for me?"

He didn't wait for her answer, not that she would have been able to form a coherent one anyway. Her clitoris throbbed, and all of her thoughts centered on coming against his mouth. His fingers trailed against her thighs and found their way to her panties. "Let's dispense with these." He tugged them down her legs as she held on to his shoulders.

Stepping back from her, he surveyed the room, his brows knitted in serious contemplation. "I need a place to feast on you." His gaze settled on the kitchen counter. "Perfect."

He lifted her onto the kitchen counter and dragged a stool in front of her. With a mischievous grin, he sat on the stool and placed her legs on his shoulders, leaving her completely open to him.

"You're so pretty here," he said as he tapped her center. "And you're ready for me to slide my tongue over your clit, aren't you?"

She squirmed on the counter. "I am, Mark. Please. Suck me now."

He used his fingers to spread her outer lips apart and then his mouth came down on her. With gentle, decisive flicks of his tongue he teased her, never coming in contact with her clit. Her clit swelled under the lack of attention as though it wanted to highlight its availability to be pleasured, too. And Karen found herself sliding her body closer to the edge of the counter, hoping that, finally, he'd place his tongue on her swollen nub.

He lifted his upper body and stared at her face, his lips glistening with traces of her. "Tell me what you need, Karen."

"I need your tongue on my clit, Mark. Please. I don't think I can wait anymore."

He obliged her, and Karen lost herself to the tiny bursts of sensation when his tongue flicked at her clit. "Oh, yes, Mark. That's it."

Humming his encouragement, he changed course and licked her slowly.

Karen dropped her head back. "Please. Suck it, too."

And he did, drawing her nub into his pursed lips and sucking softly. Karen groaned and grasped the edge of the counter as her legs shook. "Mark, don't stop, don't stop, don't stop," she chanted. Her muscles tightened in anticipation of her orgasm. And then he grazed her clit with his teeth, and the orgasm washed over her like a tidal wave. Karen squeezed her eyes shut and cried out. "Yes, Mark. Yes, yes, yes."

She came back down from her high and blinked to clear her vision. "That was incredible."

Mark raised himself from between her legs. "Are we having fun yet?"

"Definitely."

He stood and undid the first button of his shirt. "There's more fun to be had."

Karen mentally cheered that bit of good news. She *really* liked his brand of fun.

* * *

A little over a week of fun later, Karen walked into the foyer of Marcel's, an acclaimed French-Belgian restaurant in the city's Foggy Bottom neighborhood. Mark had invited her to join him for "a quick bite" after work, and she'd happily accepted his invitation.

Over the weekend, they'd flown to New York to see the American

Ballet Theatre's performance of *Swan Lake*. Karen had been spellbound by the performance, and she'd experienced a small thrill when Misty Copeland, the company's first African-American principal dancer, appeared onstage. On their return flight the next morning, Mark had peppered her with questions about her likes and dislikes, from music to foods. She'd mentioned knowing very little about French cuisine. A day later, he'd invited her to Marcel's.

She was so distracted by her thoughts, she nearly bumped into the hostess's podium. *Very smooth, Karen.* The hostess must have been trained to ignore the clientele's embarrassing behavior, because she did nothing more than greet her with a warm smile. "Mademoiselle, you have a reservation this evening?"

"I'm joining Mr. Lansing. Mark Lansing."

The hostess didn't bother to scan the reservation manifest. Instead, her eyes wandered to a spot behind Karen, and then she dipped her head and smiled—as though she were in on a secret. "Ah, yes. Your party is here already." She beckoned for Karen to follow her. "This way, please."

When they reached the end of the long corridor that would take them to the main dining area, the hostess turned to her. "Please. After you."

Karen entered the dining room, her eyes quickly adjusting to the dim lighting. The restaurant's décor surprised her. She'd expected opulence and extravagance. Instead, it epitomized understated elegance. The tables, each adorned with nothing more than a white silk tablecloth and a red glass candleholder, seemed to say, *The food is the star here, and we're just a backdrop.* The gold-framed mirrors on the walls, spaced with mathematical precision, enhanced the classic ambience of the dining room.

What surprised her the most, though, was the realization that she and Mark were the sole dinner guests in the restaurant. She slowed her approach and regarded him with her mouth open. "You arranged this?"

He stood and unbuttoned his suit jacket. "Hello to you, too."

She moved into his arms, still reeling from the arrangements he'd made. "Sorry. Hello."

He held on to her hand as she took her seat. "I thought you might enjoy a seven-course experience. That way you could decide whether you liked French food knowing you'd given it a fair shot."

"Do you know the owner or something?"

"I don't. But the restaurant is available for private dining."

"The entire restaurant?"

He nodded. "For the right price."

"But you didn't have to go to all this trouble," she said.

"No trouble. It was a phone call. Plus, I had my reasons."

"Oh, yeah. What reasons?"

"They have a top-notch sommelier. With lots of experience recommending world-class whiskeys. I figured you could try them, and if you ended up dancing on the tables, no one would know but me and the sommelier."

"You do have quite an imagination, Mark. Sounds like you're angling for a private lap dance."

He regarded her with a twinkle in his eyes. "The thought never occurred to me."

"Right."

A waiter appeared at the door to the kitchen. Mark beckoned him over. After the waiter had made the introductions and taken their selections for their seven courses, Karen reached over and held

Mark's hand. She was overwhelmed by the effort he'd put into making the evening special for her. "This is a wonderful surprise. Thank you for doing all of this."

He waved away her gratitude. "Don't give it a second thought. I promised to show you a good time. I plan to keep that promise."

Right. She reminded herself that Mark had the means to spend more money on dates than most men. What she regarded as special, he regarded as commonplace. She would do well to remember that—because forgetting would lead her to want more from Mark than she could handle.

CHAPTER EIGHTEEN

In a fit of anxiety over their upcoming move to the Maryland suburbs, Gracie and Ethan had asked Mark, Karen, and Mimi to come to join them for dinner at Gracie's apartment. So tonight, Karen and Mark's ability to keep a secret would be tested.

After checking on the roast in the oven, Gracie returned to the dining room and took her seat. "We just wanted to hang out with you guys before we become suburbanites and Ethan buys a minivan."

Ethan turned to Mark, a wide-eyed look of terror on his face. "If you see me in a minivan, shoot me and put me out of my misery."

Karen should have laughed, but with Mark a few feet away, crawling under the table to hide her distress would have been more appropriate. They'd had sex. Numerous times. Now they sat around Gracie's dining table pretending they hadn't explored each other's orifices.

She welcomed Mimi's presence. Mimi knew how to dominate a conversation, and Karen had no doubt Mimi would overshare before the night ended.

She glanced at Mark, who fingered the rim of his wineglass with two fingers. Those fingers held such promise. He glanced at her, and they froze on the glass. He turned his body toward Gracie and Ethan.

Mimi slapped her hand on the table. "Oh my God. I almost forgot. I *have* to tell you about my dream last night."

Everyone straightened and listened.

"Okay. So in the dream, I'm having some sort of identity crisis. At first, I'm not exactly sure what it is, but it's clear that I'm confused about my feelings about someone. Two women from my work take me to a bar. As I wait for the bartender to take my order, I realize that the bar is filled with nothing but women."

As though mirror images of each other, Mark and Ethan sat up and gave Mimi their undivided attention.

Mimi guffawed. "I know, right? So anyway, the setting changes and all of a sudden I'm in the desert, looking like Harrison Ford in one of those Indiana Jones movies. I mean, I'm wearing a fedora and a leather jacket and everything. And I'm searching for something but then I fall into a trap and it's dark and dingy and I have to light a match to see what's in the cave with me."

Gracie scooted her chair closer. "Oh, no. Snakes, right?"

Mimi shook her head. "No. That's just it. I light the match, and when I can finally see, there's nothing but naked men around me. And I deliver that line like I really can't stand the thought of having all these penises around me." Mimi leaned forward and sneered. "Dicks. Why did it have to be dicks?"

Gracie's shoulders shook with laughter while Ethan and Mark grinned at each other.

Karen snorted. "Oh, Mimi. Don't change. Ever."

Mimi batted her eyelashes and basked in the praise. "So maybe I'm a lesbian?"

Gracie groaned. "Dreams typically aren't that literal, Mimi. Did you have a fight with your boss again?"

Mimi pondered the question. "Now that you mention it, I did. The day before."

Gracie rose from her chair. "Well, there you go. Excuse me a minute. I'm going to check on the roast again."

Mimi took out her phone and swiped it a couple of times. "Karen. Check out my pics in Puerto Rico. The hot Marine is featured prominently."

Karen stared at the photographs, but her ears focused on Ethan and Mark's side conversation.

"So you haven't called her yet?" Ethan asked.

Mark cleared his throat. "Not yet. I've been too busy. If I'm going to approach her, I should do it when I'm not slammed at the office."

Ethan leaned back. "If?"

"Correction. When."

The finality of his words made her stomach drop. The rational part of her understood that this had been his plan all along. The irrational part of her didn't appreciate the reminder that he'd soon move on.

The scrape of Ethan's chair caused her to jump.

"I'm going to check on Gracie."

Which left Mimi, who stared longingly at the photographs of her three-day freak-a-thon. And Mark, who stared at Karen so intently, she wondered if she'd grown three heads.

"What is it?" she mouthed.

"I want you," he mouthed in return.

Oh no. Not here. *Definitely* not here.

She shook her head. "Behave," she mouthed.

He didn't acknowledge her. Instead, he pulled out his own cell phone and tapped away. "Sorry." He gestured toward his phone. "Work is always with me, unfortunately."

A buzzing from her purse made her suspicious that he'd sent a text that was not at all related to work. She fished for her phone and nearly choked when she read his text.

I want to fuck you so badly right now.

Another buzz.

That feeling of filling you to the hilt? I need that.

Her phone had turned into a vibrator.

I can't wait to see that moment of ecstasy on your face again. I've stroked my cock imagining that moment.

She moaned when she pictured him doing just that. With a huff, she typed a response.

Mimi looked up. "Something wrong?"

"No. Just getting a little hungry."

She hit Send.

What are you doing?

Yet another buzz.

I'm having fun. Don't you like foreplay?

She tapped away. *Calling it foreplay assumes we'll be having sex tonight. That's debatable.*

Mark laughed as he continued to tap at his phone. After glancing at Mimi, he bowed his head again. "Excuse me. Just something funny going on. At work."

If Karen could have reached him under the table, she would have kicked the shit out of him. But she'd get her retribution later. "All in due time."

"What?" Mimi asked.

"Um. Nothing."

Buzz.

Ethan returned, carrying the roast in a pan that had been blackened by Gracie's frequent use over the years. Gracie, looking more mussed than she did when she went into the kitchen, carried two serving plates filled with vegetables and yellow rice. "Let's eat."

They dug into the meal as they chatted about Gracie and Ethan's decorating efforts in their new home. Mimi called it a night before dessert, claiming to have a meeting with a client in the morning—on a Sunday. *Right.*

Mimi's absence meant one less person to distract her from Mark's presence. If they engaged in too much conversation, she suspected her face would reveal more than she wanted to. So she focused on dessert. "What culinary delight did you make for us?"

Gracie brushed off her shoulders. "Flan."

The family recipe for the caramel custard—which bore a striking resemblance to crème brûlée—had been passed down for four generations. Karen clapped her hands in excitement. "Can I help you get it ready?"

"No need. It's in the fridge, ready to go."

Karen gestured for Gracie to get going. "We're ready, I'd say."

Gracie rolled her eyes. "I'm going, I'm going."

When Gracie returned, she served the dessert. Ethan, meanwhile, busied himself making coffee in the kitchen.

"Have you ever tried flan before?" Gracie asked Mark.

He inspected the slice of flan. "Can't say that I have."

Karen held back a laugh at the dubious look on his face. "It's an acquired taste. Kind of like Malta."

Ethan returned with a tray of coffee mugs, having prepared cappuccinos for everyone.

"You guys are so together. Makes me sick," Karen said. She sipped her coffee and licked the froth off her top lip. "*Ooooo.* This is good. You *really* make me sick." She peeked at Mark, whose steady gaze centered on her lips.

That look warmed her insides. Made her want to snuggle with him on a couch as he sifted his fingers through her hair. Mark, she was sure, pictured a more explicit scenario.

Payback time.

She took another sip of the cappuccino and a smidge of froth clung to her lower lip. Stretching her body as though she were poised to yawn, she licked her lower lip from end to end. "*So* good. This is *really* good."

Mark's gaze narrowed. With a shake of his head, he smiled to himself and scooped a spoonful of the flan. He lifted the spoon to his mouth in slow motion.

She snuck a glance at Gracie and Ethan. The newlyweds fed each other. *Gag.* She returned her attention to Mark, who licked the spoon clean and moaned his appreciation. "Wow. That's good. So soft on my tongue. Creamy. With a touch of sweetness. I could eat this all night."

He delivered the description in his seductive baritone. Karen shifted in her seat, a telltale throb signaling that his attempt at retaliation had been far more effective than hers. When she moved, the bodice of her sundress created enough friction to cause her stiffened nipples to ache. She had to get out of here.

"I'm going to head out for the night," she said as she rose from her chair. Not bothering to wait for anyone's response, she took her plate into the kitchen and tidied up for Gracie. Her sister came in a minute later. "Leave it, Karen. Ethan and I will take care of it in the morning."

"If you're sure…"

"I am. Mark will drive you home."

Her head spun. "He will?"

"Of course. It's not a big deal, right?"

Karen shook her head. "Of course not. I'll just grab my purse."

A few minutes later, she and Mark walked out of Gracie's apartment.

"Bye, you two," Gracie called after him.

Karen rushed down the stairs. Mark followed close behind. So close the heat emanating from his body warmed her skin. She reached for the doorknob, but he pulled her back into the vestibule and maneuvered her against the wall.

Her body melded to his as he swooped down for a kiss. Their lips came together with no semblance of finesse. He capped off the kiss by tugging on her bottom lip, and she welcomed the resulting prick of pain. They broke apart and gulped in air, their chests heaving in the aftermath.

"That was torture." He held her hand and placed it over his crotch. "You did this to me. If we'd stayed one minute longer, I would have taken you in the bathroom."

His words unleashed a fire that started in her belly and spread everywhere, its hottest spot centered on her core. She couldn't stand it any longer. "Mark."

"Yeah, baby."

"I'm so wet. I don't think I can wait. I…"

He wrapped his hand around the back of her neck and pulled her face within centimeters of his. "Tell me. What do you need?"

"I need you to fuck me. Now."

His eyes snapped shut. "Hang on." He reached in his back pocket and produced a condom. Impatient and greedy, she ripped the foil packet from his hands and opened it. He pulled his zipper down and fisted his cock, beads of sweat dotting his nose and forehead. When she rolled the condom on, he threw his head back and slammed his hand against the wall.

She reached for her panties, but he stopped her, pushing them to the side instead. "No time."

When he pushed inside her, Karen threw her head back and scraped her nails against the wall. He lifted one of her legs and gripped it at the back of her knee. For once, she didn't care that she was splayed out in a public place. At that moment she only cared about him filling her—to the hilt as he'd promised. And when he did, Karen's head fell back against the wall, and she squeezed her eyes shut to concentrate on the fullness inside her. She grabbed his waist and braced herself for each fierce stroke, crying out each time he slammed into her.

They moved together at full speed, a push and a pull, a rhythm that alternated between staccato notes and long, continuous ones. Her hands searched for him, her vision clouded by the sensations coursing through her. She snaked her hand around the nape of his neck and grabbed a fistful of hair, yanking his head back so she could suck on the skin below his jaw. Within seconds, his muscles tightened under her hands, as though her touch had stretched his body to its breaking point. Never severing their connection, he bent his knees slightly, lifted her against the wall by her butt, and drove upward.

Karen used her hand to muffle the scream that bubbled at the back of her throat. Over and over he plunged, his mouth inches away from hers, his hooded gaze focused on her face. "Touch yourself, sweetheart."

In a haze, she moved her hand to her clit and teased herself, skating over the slick flesh several times before pressing her fingers against it. She rubbed slow and hard, teetering on the edge, her toes curling in her shoes.

"That's it, baby," he said against her ear. "Rub your clit for me."

"Oh, God. I'm tingling everywhere."

She pressed harder. He stroked deeper. She was *so* close, she wanted to scream in frustration. Mark's thrusts stretched her, his cock filling her completely and leaving no space untouched. Karen savored the sensation of fullness.

They came within seconds of each other, their moans and grunts mingling and echoing in the cavernous space.

Karen regained her equilibrium and surveyed her surroundings. She'd just had sex against a wall in the vestibule of her sister's apartment building. Mark was definitely a bad influence on her. Even worse, she couldn't muster enough energy to do anything about it.

CHAPTER NINETEEN

A week after the wall banging, the fun times came to a grinding halt.

As she paced the length of Mark's master bathroom, Karen fought the urge to puke. Dammit. A rush of heat blasted her face, and she fanned herself in an unsuccessful attempt to wave it away.

Oh, God. She was so freaking hot. The promise of an ice cold shower tempted her. Would Mark mind if she jumped in fully clothed? Probably not. But if she did that, he'd think she was crazy. Okay, the next best thing would be to douse her face in cold tap water. She pulled her hair back and bent over the sink bowl. A few splashes and she'd be as good as new, she told herself. But when she stood, a wave of dizziness attacked her, and she fell flat on her ass.

Mark banged on the door. "Karen? What's going on?"

She cleared her throat and called out to him, but her vocal chords protested her efforts. A wad of Brillo might as well have been lodged in there. She mangled his name, of course, and struggled to form the words to tell him she was okay. After a few false starts, she rose from the floor and opened the bathroom door.

Mark placed his hands on her shoulders, his gaze cataloging her face. "Karen, look at me. Are you okay?"

She shook her head. "No. I think I have the flu."

Now that she thought about it, the guy who'd sat next to her in the library a few days earlier had coughed and shivered a lot. She'd assumed he was reacting to the frigid temperature of the room. The possibility that he was sick had never occurred to her, so she'd placed her headphones on her head and continued to study. Who gets sick in the summer anyway? she wondered. *He did, you dumbass.* And now she was sick, too. So much for needing more condoms. What she needed was a sweat rag.

So very sexy. Oof.

* * *

Karen woke up in Mark's bed, an enormous contraption with a black four-poster canopy frame and a mattress covered with sumptuous midnight blue sheets.

She lifted the sheet. Mark had removed her clothes and dressed her in one of his oversized T-shirts. It smelled clean and fresh, just like him, and she wrapped her arms around herself, comforted by the knowledge that he'd taken care of her.

She sat up. Whoa. Her body ached everywhere. She collapsed against the mattress and listened for any sign that Mark was in the vicinity. But his condo was quiet—eerily so. A glass of water sat on the steel-framed bedside table. She guzzled it.

"Feeling better?" a voice said from the far corner of the room.

Karen jumped—and the sudden movement caused her to spill the water down the front of his T-shirt. "Dammit, Mark," she said as she wiped the water away. "You scared me."

"Sorry," he said as he rose from a chaise lounge partially hidden by a half wall. He emerged from the shadows like an action hero: bare-chested and purposeful, his jeans riding low on his hips. He held a book in his hand. *Definitely* her kind of action hero.

"How do you feel?" he asked.

She smacked her lips, her mouth moving as though it were filled with cotton. "Groggy and thirsty. Thanks for letting me crash here. Not sure I would have been able to make it home."

He cocked his head, and a line appeared between his brows. "Why would you have needed to go home? You already agreed to stay."

She picked at the nonexistent lint on his duvet cover. "I just figured you'd want to keep clear of me. I'm sick so…"

The crease between his brows disappeared as understanding dawned on his face. "So you thought because we wouldn't be having sex, I'd want you gone."

She looked up at him. "Something like that."

"Well, you're not wrong," he said with a smile. "I was just waiting for your sorry ass to wake up so I could throw you out." His voice was laced with laughter, which immediately set her at ease.

She grabbed the pillow behind her and threw it at him. "I'll get out of your hair then."

His smile turned into a frown. "No. You'll stay."

"Why? Because…me…Jane…and you…Tarzan?"

He rolled his eyes. "Because you're not well. You need to hydrate.

You need to eat. And you need lots of rest. You need someone to take care of you."

She raised her eyebrows, sure that she was setting herself up for premature wrinkles. "And you're that person."

"Absolutely," he said as he crossed his arms over his chest. "You doubt my capabilities?"

"In most areas, no," she said as she glanced at his crotch. "To nurse me back to health? Yes."

"Well, I plan to show you that your doubts are unfounded. I'm working from home the next few days, until you're feeling better. Get used to me taking care of you. I'll be doing it twenty-four/seven until you're well."

The thought of him taking care of her twenty-four/seven made her giddy inside, but she was so freaking exhausted she couldn't even smile. "I feel like I've been hit by a Mack truck. Excuse me while I sleep for the rest of the week."

"Wait," he said as he picked up her cell phone from the nightstand. He handed it to her. "Can you text Gracie and let her know you're okay?"

"Sure."

She sent Gracie a quick text letting her know she wasn't feeling well and would be hibernating a few days.

Gracie responded immediately asking if she needed anything, to which she replied that she was all set with soup and ice cream. Before she closed her eyes, she caught the view of Mark's jean-clad butt as he left his bedroom. She groaned. The flu might not kill her, but that man's ass would certainly be the death of her.

* * *

She awoke to the smell of bacon. So this was heaven, huh?

For the first time since she'd been felled by the flu, she examined her surroundings. He'd decorated his bedroom with utility in mind. The furniture consisted of just four items: the bed, the chaise lounge in the far right corner, and the bedside tables. And the silk drapes blocked any sunlight from entering the room. He slept in this room, perhaps read in it from time to time, but it revealed nothing about the man who owned this home. She found that strange. And sad.

He padded into the room barefoot, a silver tray in his hands. "Good morning. I have bacon, toast, and a scrambled egg for you. Think you're up for it?"

She nodded vigorously and rubbed her hands together. "I'm starving." He placed the tray on her lap, and she inspected it with greedy eyes. "You made all this?"

"Absolutely." He paused. "Not."

She stared at him. "Personal chef, eh?"

"She comes in twice a week to make meals and put them in the freezer. She made this breakfast at my special request."

"Thank you," she managed in between chews of the bacon.

"How are you feeling?"

"Better. My throat is sore."

"I have tea and honey for that."

"And my body still aches. But I'm not hot."

"Your fever broke last night, hence the tank top."

She looked down at her clothing and wrinkled her nose. "I need a shower stat."

"Yes, yes, you do," he said with a twinkle in his eye.

She spied a chair filled with various items. "What's all this?"

"I got you a few things. A robe. I went with pink, but if you hate it, I can arrange to get it in white. A few magazines. I had no idea whether you like fashion magazines or news magazines, so I got you a few different ones."

She pointed at a textbook. "What's that?"

"So I figured you might want to use this time to brush up on anatomy. First-year med students have to take that class, I gather. You'll be dissecting a cadaver, right?"

She lost her appetite at the thought and set the last strip of bacon back on her plate. "Yes."

"This Netter book seems to be the gold standard."

The gesture truly overwhelmed her. She was used to her family doing thoughtful things for her, but a man had never purchased anything for her simply because he wanted to. Her breath hitched before she could express her gratitude. "Mark. That's perfect. And Netter is on my book list. It was out of stock when I tried to purchase it."

"I'm glad it'll be useful." He placed his hands in his jeans pockets. "So I've got a conference call at ten. Will you be okay on your own?"

She lifted the glass of orange juice to her lips and gestured for him to hand her the anatomy book. "I'm going to take a shower and then I'll study. Don't worry about me."

He stared at her for a few seconds; any more than that would have taken them to awkward town. With a shake of his head, he handed her the book, and then he left, closing the door softly behind him.

She fell back against the mattress and hugged her pillow. Soon, she'd start medical school, and there'd be no looking back after that. Her attention was a precious thing, and she had none to spare for a relationship. Still, a part of her wished they could continue what they'd started, without defining their relationship or placing any limits on where it would go. And that scared her.

She'd told him not to worry about her. There was no need, really, because she had enough worries to cover them both.

CHAPTER TWENTY

Four days. She'd stayed with him for four days.

Not a single kiss. Not a single touch. Nothing. He'd been okay with it then—he knew how to control his horniness for the sake of her health—but if he'd had to walk into his bedroom one more night, the sweet scent of her filling his nostrils as soon as he crossed the threshold, he would have jerked off in the bathroom like he was back in middle school. *No magazines required.*

Mark grimaced at the trajectory of his thoughts. Great. Now she'd turned him into a man with no self-control. Disgusted with himself, he turned to his computer with the intention of reading the dozens of e-mails that had come in this morning alone. A few minutes later, Karen slipped through the door unannounced. Her bouncy hair and sweet smile brightened his office and lifted his spirits.

"Hey, there," she said with a smile. "Don't be mad at Nicole. I asked her if I could surprise you."

He closed out of his e-mail account and gave her a wide smile. "This is a nice surprise."

She came closer to his desk and licked her lips. "So I…uh…I wanted to thank you, for taking care of me."

Only then did he notice she held a paper bag in her hands. "What do you have in there?"

Her grin lit up her entire face. "Lunch. Courtesy of DC Empanadas in Union Market. I bring you an assortment of fried, yummy goodness."

A man could only hold back for so long. They had unfinished business after all. "That's very kind of you, but you're all the yummy goodness I need."

Her brown eyes went smoky. "Oh, yeah?"

"Yeah."

She walked toward him and set the bag and her purse on the far corner of his desk. No matter how innocent she'd intended her visit to be, it was clear they now needed privacy. He reached for the remote to lock his office door while she rounded his desk. She hiked her dress up and gave him a tantalizing peek at her thighs before she faced him and sat on his lap. In the process of adjusting herself, she grazed his cock with her hand, and it stiffened at the contact.

His gaze flew to her face, where a mischievous smile revealed she hadn't grazed his dick by accident. "Someone's in a teasing mood, I see."

She placed a hand on her chest, widened her eyes, and feigned innocence. "Whatever do you mean?"

In answer, he slipped the spaghetti straps off her shoulders and tugged the top half of her dress to her waist. Her bra, a lacy number with scalloped edges that ended well below the tops of her breasts, resembled a frothy pink treat. The sheer cups revealed the outline of her brown nipples. The thought of sucking on them made him hard. Real fucking hard.

Unable to restrain himself, he buried his face in the space between her breasts, and then placed openmouthed kisses along the cups of her bra. She undulated on his thighs and pressed her breasts closer to his mouth. "God, I've wanted this so much."

"Believe me, you're not the only one," he said between soft kisses.

She reached for the clasp of her bra.

"Leave your hands on my shoulders, please. I'm not ready for that yet."

She groaned. "This will come back to bite you in the butt, you know."

"Is that what you're into these days?"

She dropped her head into the crook of his neck and nipped at him.

He used his tongue to lave her nipples through the bra. A soft "oh" escaped her lips. He studied her face, captivated by the way her mouth fell open, soft and wet. "Tell me what you want, sweetheart."

She opened her eyes and her gaze landed everywhere but on him.

"Listen to me, Karen. The sound of your voice turns me on. Everything about you turns me inside out. Tell me what you want. I guarantee you, whatever you say will be perfect."

She brushed a tendril of hair away from her face and nodded. "I…Mark…I need your cock in me. I just want to feel you pump inside me over and over. Right now."

His dick swelled at her words. This would happen just as she wanted it to. He lifted her off him and set her on his desk; she spread her legs for him and tugged him close. Then her hands dropped to his waist, where she worked quickly to undo his belt and pull down his slacks. She reached into her purse and produced a condom like she'd pulled a rabbit out of a hat.

Her roaming hands stilled. "Tada, indeed. Were you planning all along to give me more than an empanada?"

"Nope. I carry them everywhere I go. Always prepared. That's my motto."

"Well, I'm so fucking glad you had one."

She dropped her head against his shoulder. "So am I."

He didn't care for any more conversation. Not this time. After sheathing himself, he removed her shoes and reached for her panties. Finding none, he groaned. "You went commando?"

"I'd like to think of it as going G.I. Jane."

He leaned forward and smiled into her neck. His hands wrapped around her ass and he pulled her to the edge of the desk. Then he centered himself at her entrance and pushed inside. "You're so fucking tight."

"Because you're so fucking big."

"And you love it."

"I do. I *really, really* do."

He pushed farther inside, wincing when her nails dug into his back. He grabbed on to her waist and pushed harder, each stroke deeper than the last. Her sounds of pleasure coached him, urging him through her moans and heavy breathing to help her reach an explosive orgasm. He wanted that for her—badly. Just as badly as he wanted it for himself.

With each thrust of her hips, her moans grew louder. Still cognizant of where they were, he covered her lips with his, taking her sounds into his mouth as though they were his own. His balls grew heavy and tight, the climax so close. He placed two fingers on her clit and rubbed her. She whimpered, and then her body shook from the force of her orgasm, her hand slapping his desk repeatedly as the wave of pleasure hit her. He didn't take long to join her. Two strokes in, his release slammed into him, and he found himself unsteady on his feet as he rode it out.

He snapped his eyes shut and shook his head. She rested against him, breathing fast and heavy.

"That was incredible," he said as he threw the condom in the trash. "If that's what I can expect when you visit me for lunch, feel free to show up every day."

Like an electric shock, the words he'd uttered sank into his psyche and zapped him of his coordination. He fumbled with the zipper of his slacks. *Fuck.* Now he'd gone and done the unthinkable: He'd let his mind trick him into thinking their short-term arrangement had blossomed into something more.

She rose, her movements slow and unsure. Her gaze never leaving his, she slipped her arms through the spaghetti straps and smoothed the skirt of her dress. "Your empanadas are probably cold."

He rolled up his sleeves. "I'll live. Thanks for bringing them."

Her soft smile reminded him of the shy woman he'd spent time with in Puerto Rico.

"Just remember," she said. "I came to bring you lunch." Pointing between them, she continued, "You're the one who turned it into this."

"So noted."

She puffed out a breath and grabbed her purse. "Okay. I'm off to finish buying books for my first semester."

The urge to *do something* made him call out her name. "Karen, before you go, I need to talk to you about something."

She turned to face him and regarded him with wariness in her eyes. "What's up?"

"It's Gracie and Ethan. They've been pressing me to go on dates, and I'm running out of excuses for why I'm never available. And well, the more I think about this…us, I think it would be a good idea if I contacted the woman they have in mind. It'll get them off my back, for one thing. For another thing, you're starting medical school soon, so…"

His voice trailed off, and she finished the sentence for him. "So you should get started on your plans to find Mrs. Lansing, right?"

"Well, that's skipping a few steps, but that's the basic idea. I just wanted you to know. Like you said before, just so there's no confusion. I didn't want you to think I was being dishonest about my intentions."

"Oh no, Mark. I'd never accuse you of dishonesty. You've been painfully honest every step of the way."

He nodded, ignoring the way she'd stressed the word *painfully*. "Okay."

She massaged her temples. "So are we done, or do you still want to see me?"

"It's up to you."

She licked the front of her teeth and stared out his office window. "I think as long as we both know what's going on here, there's no reason to stop…" Her brow furrowed, likely because she was searching for the right words.

He didn't know how to define what they were doing, either, but he knew he didn't want to stop. Not yet. "I agree with you. Just so we're all clear."

"Okay."

"Okay," he echoed.

She dropped her chin. "One thing, though."

"Anything."

"Well, I just don't feel comfortable with the idea that you'd be having sex with her, too. So if you—"

"Karen, there's no way I'd do that. You can be one hundred percent sure of that."

"All right. Well, if things change, just tell me. I can be mature about this."

"Okay."

"Tomorrow night then?"

"Sure. That works."

She strode toward him, appearing mussed and thoroughly sated. Her gaze bore into his before she kissed his lips. "Thanks for a lovely time."

She'd said it like a woman thanking a man on their first date. Like she didn't know him well, and didn't care to. It didn't matter, he reasoned. He'd eke out whatever pleasure he could get from their remaining time together and move on. And although it would hurt him to let her go, he knew it was the right thing to do.

CHAPTER TWENTY-ONE

The first day of med school was only a week away.

Although she'd managed to wade through half of Netter's *Atlas of Human Anatomy*, the only anatomy that captured her attention came in the form of a strapping, two-hundred-pound man who paced his living room. She'd come to learn that he sorted out work matters on the move, unable to sit in a chair for very long.

Wearing one of his dress shirts and nothing else, Karen swiveled the counter stool and positioned herself to admire him. After a few seconds, he froze and whipped his head up in her direction. He planted himself in the middle of the room with his arms crossed over his bare chest. His jeans, unbuttoned and zipped halfway, hung low on his hips. The patch of hair below his waist teased her, because she knew what she'd find at the end of that happy trail, and she also knew she only had a limited time in which to enjoy it.

She'd lost focus for another reason, too. Mark had been unavailable two nights this week. Nothing about that fact struck her as out of the ordinary, but when she'd asked him about his plans, he'd sidestepped her question. She needed to know—no matter how hard it would be to stomach his response. "So did you meet with that woman Gracie and Ethan set you up with?"

He rubbed the back of his neck and cleared his throat. "Yeah."

Shit. Why did that hurt so fucking much? Maybe she couldn't do this. "What's her name?"

He tilted his head in her direction. "You really want to know?"

She shrugged. "Sure, why not? I'm not a psycho, Mark. I'm not going to boil a rabbit in her house or anything. It's cool."

He sat on the stool next to her, his gaze fixed on the digital clock in his kitchen. "Her name's Sharon Castellano." He grabbed a sheaf of papers on the kitchen counter and straightened them. "This is weird, Karen. Suffice it to say we had a decent time. Hard to say where it'll lead."

"Fair enough. Just asking. Didn't mean to make you feel uncomfortable."

"Let's forget about it, okay?"

"It's forgotten."

That night they went to bed with space between them, a marked change from their usual spooning positions.

It was for the best, wasn't it? Soon they wouldn't share any space at all.

* * *

No matter how hard she tried, Karen couldn't stop picturing Mark on his date with Sharon Castellano. To make matters worse, Gracie had invited her to a home design center, to get her opinion on a slab of granite for the kitchen island in Gracie and Ethan's new home.

Boredom and jealousy made for a very unpleasant mix. If Karen was lucky, a runaway slab of granite would slam into her head and knock her unconscious.

Her first mistake had been to ask Mark about the date. While she pretended to be unconcerned about it, last night's seemingly offhand inquiry had occupied her thoughts ever since. He'd said the date was decent, but what else *could* he say? She was open to discussing his attempts at dating, but she suspected that if any of those dates went well, Mark wouldn't flaunt that fact in her face. She should have feigned disinterest and left the subject alone.

Gracie sprinted to the next slab of granite. "*Oooh.* This one's beautiful. What do you think?"

Karen stared at the slab and shrugged. "It's nice?"

Gracie lifted her head toward the ceiling of the showroom. "Why did I ask you to come with me again?"

"Because no one else is crazy enough to do this with you?"

Gracie turned her attention to the slab once more. "Right. Thanks for the reminder."

Karen figured this was as good a time as any to do some sleuthing. "So how are things going on the matchmaking front? For Mark, I mean."

Distracted by her careful inspection of her favorite slab so far, Gracie didn't bother to meet Karen's gaze when she responded. "We've gotten nowhere, no thanks to Mark. The man's so busy, we can't get him to call the lady."

"You have someone specific in mind?"

"Yeah. A former co-worker of mine. Sharon Castellano. But Mark keeps making excuses. And now she's away on vacation in Australia, so they're probably not going to connect for a few weeks.

Before she left, though, she said she hoped she'd hear from him soon."

"Oh, he hasn't even contacted her?"

"He couldn't have. She's been off the grid at a business retreat." Gracie looked up at her then. "Why all the questions?"

Karen forced herself not to stutter. "Oh, just wondering. I'm thinking I might know someone who'd be perfect for him."

Gracie's eyes widened with interest. "Yeah?"

"Maybe. Let me think about it some more. If he's not enthused about doing this, I wouldn't want to get the woman's hopes up for nothing."

"Exactly. So far Mark hasn't been enthusiastic at all. It's like he's stalling or something, which is strange given that he was the one to come to Ethan about this. It's all very confusing. I've been meaning to confront him about it, but I think Ethan's the best person to do that."

Karen disagreed. *She* was the best person to confront Mark about it, and she intended to do just that.

CHAPTER TWENTY-TWO

Mark stared out his office window and brooded. He hated lying to Karen, but if they wanted a clean break from each other, the lie would help them accomplish it. Then she'd go off to medical school. And he'd contact Sharon Castellano—for real. The plan was simple, but it wasn't easy to execute.

His assistant buzzed him. "Mark, your dad's here."

Great. He'd completely forgotten about the other development that had made him edgy. This morning his father had asked to see him. In the city. Both of those facts concerned him. His father came to see him only rarely, and he hated the city. Whatever had drawn him out of his self-imposed exile meant bad news. He was sure of it.

Mark massaged his chest and braced himself for whatever his father's visit would bring. So when his father waltzed through his office door, Mark couldn't have been more surprised by the man who greeted him. He appeared to be happy. In fact, he'd taken extra care with his attire, and he'd styled his hair differently—meaning he'd actually combed it instead of relying on his customary harried professor hairdo.

His father shook his hand with confidence. "It's good to see you, son."

"Same here."

"May I sit?"

Mark gestured to one of the chairs facing his desk. "Of course." He waited for his father to settle into his seat. Just barely, though. "So what's going on? The last time we saw each other in the city was ages ago, and you came under protest."

"I have news. Your mother and I are making a second go of it."

Mark stared at his father. "A second go of what, exactly?"

"A second go of our relationship. We're getting back together."

He couldn't help being moved by his father's expectant gaze. Was his father seeking his approval? That would be ridiculous—and unnecessary. His father was an adult, after all, and Mark's views on a reconciliation between his parents was beside the point. "Is this what you want?"

"Of course it's what I want. She's not forcing me to take her back. I'm not under duress, if that's what you're asking."

"Okay, okay. Well, what's the plan? When will you see each other? Is she moving in with you? Are you moving closer to her?"

"Slow down, Mark. We're not picking out our china and silverware just yet. We're dating. Getting to know each other again. Trying to see if we're still compatible."

"How long has this been going on?"

"Several weeks now."

Several weeks ago his mother had contacted him about Spencer.

She must have reached out to his father shortly after that. "And things are good?"

"Things are great. She's a different woman, and I happen to like the woman she's become."

"Well, then I'm happy for you. But you didn't have to come to the city to tell me this. A phone call would have sufficed, though I appreciate the effort."

"It was your mother's idea. Plus, she wanted me to take her to lunch, so I figured I could do both in one trip."

"Where is she now?"

A rap at the door answered Mark's question. Seconds later, his mother sailed into his office. He glanced at his father, who suddenly found the pattern of the office's carpet enthralling.

She glided across the room, enveloped his hands in hers, and gave them a firm squeeze. "Mark, so good to see you, dear."

His mother's dark beauty hadn't faded since he'd seen her in this very office four years ago. She wore her dark brown hair in a blunt cut, and the light touch of makeup she used enhanced her doe eyes.

"Good to see you, Lisa."

His father cleared his throat and squished his eyes together.

"Oh, don't be cross with him, Paul. I asked him not to call me 'mother.'" She waved her hands in the air—because her dismissive tone hadn't been enough, apparently. "It's just never been my thing."

Mark clamped his mouth shut, a well-placed derisive comment on the tip of his tongue. What would be the point? His mother had made the effort to reconnect with his father—and judging by her presence today, she wanted the same opportunity to reconnect with him.

Maybe he'd misunderstood her motivations all these years. After all, he'd only been a kid when she walked away from her marriage, and he had no way of knowing if the marriage had been rocky for other reasons—reasons having to do with his father, even. The simple and mature response would be to wish them well.

His father leaned forward, his knees bouncing. "You're sure you're okay with this, son?"

For as long as he could remember, he and his father had operated as a unit—sometimes a dysfunctional unit but a unit nonetheless. So it made sense that his father would worry about his reaction. But he hadn't meant his silence to alarm his father. "Dad, go take Mo—take *Lisa* to lunch and have fun." He walked to the door, hoping to usher them out.

His mother looked up at his father. "See? I told you there was nothing to worry about. Now you know for sure."

Lisa placed her hand under Mark's chin and blew his an air kiss. "Bye, dear." She swept out of the office, his father trailing a few steps behind her. Before his father walked out the door, he turned back. "Look, I know your mother and I might not make sense on paper, but it's been a while since I've taken a leap and just trusted my feelings. Sometimes your heart knows a lot more than your head."

With that morsel of wisdom out of the way, his father walked out the door, leaving him in a state of confusion.

* * *

After asking Gracie to release her from the torture of granite and tile selections, Karen stormed into Mark's office, not bothering to stop at his assistant's reception desk.

Nicole, Mark's assistant, trailed behind her, begging Karen to let her announce her unscheduled arrival.

Karen nevertheless strode across his office and stood in front of his desk. "You lied to me."

Behind her, Nicole jumped into the conversation. "I'm sorry, Mr. Lansing. She caught me off guard."

He kept his gaze on his computer screen. "It's okay, Nicole. I'll handle this."

Nicole walked out muttering about crazy girlfriends and the lack of a job description requiring her to deal with them. Karen would apologize later. For now, she had a man to skewer.

Mark swiveled his chair in her direction and pushed his glasses up to the bridge of his nose. He resembled Clark Kent in one of those moments when only an idiot couldn't guess that he was Superman.

"You wear glasses?" she asked.

He whipped them off. "For reading only."

"You look good in them." She shook her head. *Gah. He was so distracting.* "Back to what I'm pissed about. You lied to me."

He leaned back in his chair and rested his elbows on the arms, creating a steeple with his fingers as he settled into the seat. "About what?"

She mimicked his aloof demeanor. "About what? You know about what. You never went on a date with Sharon Castellano."

His face blanched. "Who told you that?"

"Gracie."

"Gracie doesn't follow my every waking moment, you know."

"Yes, but she knows that Sharon Castellano's at a business retreat. *In Australia.* And before she left, she told Gracie she hadn't heard from you."

He rose and sat on the edge of his desk. "Okay, yes. I lied to you."

"Because?"

"Because I think we're getting closer than either of us anticipated, and I needed to do something to remind myself of the end game."

She dropped into one of the chairs facing his desk. "Why does there have to be an end game? We're enjoying each other's company. Does it have to be anything more than that? I don't expect marriage. I don't even expect a long-term commitment. But I do expect honesty, and for whatever reason, we've reached the point where you can't be honest with me."

His shoulders sagged. "You're right."

Finally. A breakthrough. "And?"

He sighed. "And if you want more honesty, I'm being pulled in more directions than I care to keep track of. Gracie and Ethan keep pushing me to meet someone, which I can't really fault them for since I asked for their help. But I'm lying to them, pretending I'm too busy to meet with that woman when I know something else is holding me back. And then there's you. And whatever it is we're doing here. Oh. And I'm running a company where my top managers seem to perpetually have their heads in their asses. It's a lot to manage."

She leaned forward and squeezed his thigh. "I'm sorry you're feeling so stressed. This isn't easy for me, either, you know. I hadn't figured on wanting to spend more time with you."

He studied her. "That's what you want? To spend more time with me?"

"Yes."

His eyes softened. "I want that, too."

"So we're dating?"

He stood and pulled her out of the chair. "Yeah, we're dating."

"And Sharon Castellano is out of the picture?" she asked as she snuggled into him.

"Karen, she was never *in* the picture. She's been photoshopped out of my life, okay?"

"Okay."

Karen smiled. They might not be a perfect match, but she wanted to be with him anyway. So no more second-guessing her feelings, no more worrying about what-ifs. Besides, how bad could things possibly get?

CHAPTER TWENTY-THREE

After the start of Karen's classes, she and Mark settled into a comfortable routine. They spent a couple of nights together each week, typically at Mark's place and occasionally at Karen's apartment.

Because Mark didn't bring home work often, when she studied, he hovered in the background, watching an NFL game or listening to music. Sometimes she'd catch him staring at her as she reviewed her lecture notes. Today was no different.

Standing behind her, he leaned over and spoke close to her ear. "What are you studying?"

She jumped at the contact and closed the book. "Human gross anatomy."

He winced. "Is it gross?"

She rolled her eyes. "*Ba-dum-bum.* This class is going to kick my butt."

"It just started. How can you tell?"

"The professor's big on making her students compete for everything. As an incentive to study, you don't get to work with your group's cadaver unless you get above eighty percent on your first exam. And our midterms are based on our dissections of the cadavers, so if you have less time to work with it, you're going in to the midterm exam with a significant disadvantage."

"That's brutal."

"That's medical school."

He placed his hands on her shoulders and kneaded them. "You've got this."

"After I study a bajillion hours, I'll be able to agree with you."

"Can you spare me a few hours this weekend?"

Karen narrowed her eyes. "A few?"

"Okay, you got me. I need the whole weekend. I have a surprise for you. I'd planned it for the week you were hit with the flu, but as you know, I spent several days nursing you back to health instead."

He said this with fake woe-is-me expression on his face. Karen wanted to say no, but the reminder that he'd taken care of her that week made her feel guilty about it. Mark seemed to know that she was conflicted about it, since he added, "You can study on the flight there and back."

"All right. I'll go. *Just the weekend*, right?"

"Right. I promise it'll be worth it."

Given that she was giving up much-needed study time before her first exam in medical school, she certainly hoped so.

* * *

Mark's surprise was a visit to wine country in Willamette Valley, Oregon. She'd never been to the Pacific Northwest, a fact she'd shared with Mark when he'd taken her to New York weeks ago.

He'd reserved a room at a local bed-and-breakfast a few miles away from several wineries. The lush grounds of the B and B invited its guests to relax, and Karen and Mark enjoyed their tranquil surroundings by taking hikes and picnicking among the cedar trees in the B and B's orchard. Mark's penchant for excitement would not be denied, however, so he'd also planned an adventure, but he wouldn't tell Karen anything about it.

The last day of the trip, Mark woke her before dawn. "Wake up, sleepyhead. We have to get going."

Karen yawned and sat up. Mark, who'd rushed to get dressed, paused as he stepped into his cargo pants and leaned over for a kiss. "You look incredible there."

She'd draped a sheet around her naked body, and her hair hung around her shoulders. "If I look so incredible here, why don't we just stay here?"

His gaze was as soft as a caress. "Tempting, but I don't want you to miss this. I think it'll be an unforgettable experience."

She couldn't imagine what he'd planned, so she rushed to get ready, a sense of giddiness making her move at twice her normal speed.

* * *

"We're going on a hot air balloon ride?"

Mark pulled her to the launch site. "Yes. Up for it?"

Um. She wasn't sure. The balloons appeared a lot smaller than she'd imagined. And there wouldn't be much of a barrier between her and the ground below. "Couldn't I just watch from here?"

Mark's eyes shone with excitement. "It'll be great, and I'll be with you."

She looked at him with a straight face, doing her best to signal that she didn't find his promise to be with her impressive. "Unless you have wings, Mark, your presence isn't all that comforting."

He embraced her and nipped at her neck. "You can do this."

"All right. Let's go before I change my mind."

Karen and Mark helped stretch out the balloon. The safety personnel then inflated the balloon and did the requisite safety checks. Mark helped Karen climb into the balloon; a few minutes later the balloon rose into the air.

Karen closed her eyes at first, but ten feet in the air, she opened her eyes. "Wow. Just wow." Still clutching Mark's arm, she spun around as the distance between the ground and the balloon increased.

"How do you feel?" Mark asked.

"Overwhelmed. You can hardly feel the wind, and the morning haze makes the valley look magical."

The balloon followed the direction of the wind, seemingly becoming one with it. They floated above wineries and the Willamette River, and the pilot even navigated the balloon so that it skimmed the river.

Mark caged her in his arms as she held on to the balloon's basket. "It was a scary start, right? But isn't this worth it?"

She turned in to him, pushing her hair behind her ears. "Yes and yes."

"Remember this feeling, Karen, when medical school threatens to overwhelm you."

She rested the back of her head against his chest, a deep sense of calm washing over her. "I will."

He'd put a lot of thought into this trip, and while she hadn't gotten as much studying as she would have liked, she didn't regret her decision to join him.

Not yet.

CHAPTER TWENTY-FOUR

The Saturday after Karen's first med school exam, she sprang an impromptu gathering on him. "A few students from my study group are getting together tonight," she told him. "To celebrate the end of the first exam period. I made plans to catch up with them at Bourbon in Adams Morgan. Want to join me?"

The idea of hanging out with a bunch of medical students—in a bar, no less—held zero appeal for him. "I'll pass."

Karen snuggled into him and rested her chin on his chest. "Come on. Just an hour or two," she said, her voice playful. When he didn't respond, she shook him and pretended to pout. "Pretty please? It'll be fun."

"Your idea of fun is very different from mine. I'm a little too old to be hanging out with a bunch of med students."

She backed up and pursed her lips. "Wow. Sorry I asked. I didn't realize wanting to grab a drink with friends and, oh, I don't know, *talking with them*, would make us star-crossed lovers. It's not like I was suggesting we hang out at a frat house. And for your information, some of them are your age."

He pulled her back into his arms. "I'm not in the mood to go out tonight. It's as simple as that. That's what I should have said when you asked."

"Fine," she said in a clipped tone.

He'd averted a crisis. Next time he would choose his words more carefully. He rested his chin on her head and rubbed her back. Arms at her side—and still pissed, apparently—Karen stood in the circle of his arms like deadweight. He stepped back and lifted her chin. "Is there anything I can do to make it up to you?"

She shifted in place, her dim eyes staring back at him. "I have to head back to my place. To change." She pasted on a smile. "Have fun doing"—she waved her hands in the air—"whatever it is rich single men do on a Saturday night."

She grabbed her purse and walked out the door, closing it softly. He would have preferred for her to slam the door shut instead. A slammed door meant he'd angered her, but a soft click of the lock was much worse in his mind; it meant he'd hurt her.

An hour later, he ran at a brisk pace along Connecticut Avenue. To clear his head, he told himself. But his thoughts centered on Karen, and he couldn't outrun them no matter how much he tried. He pictured her at Bourbon, chatting with friends and enjoying herself. He wanted that for her.

Mark ran over a mile before he realized he'd crossed into Adams Morgan, a neighborhood dubbed "quirky" and "eclectic" by travel guides. A hotspot for weekend activities, the area attracted a diverse crowd, from hipsters to suits to college students, but a single man running through the streets at sunset still raised a few brows. As if such a man were suspicious by virtue of the fact that he had no plans to frequent a bar or dine in a restaurant. Why else would one be here after all?

He asked himself the same question when he found himself in front of Bourbon's entrance. Yes, he might regret showing up unannounced, but the possibility that he'd hurt her feelings earlier propelled him up the steps anyway.

The silver-suited bouncer, a beefy guy with a blond Mohawk, greeted him at the top of the steps. Thor eyed Mark's running attire and raised a hand like a crossing guard. "Not going to happen, buddy. We have a dress code."

"I'm not staying," Mark said as he reached inside the pocket of his shorts for his billfold. "I just need to check on someone and then I'm gone." He held up a hundred-dollar bill. "Are we cool?"

The bouncer looked at the bill and waved him through. "I expect to see you soon," he said as he plucked the money from Mark's hand.

"No worries. You will."

Mark surveyed the main level but didn't spot her. He'd been here before, years ago, so he knew there were two other levels where she could be. Two minutes into his search, he found her on the second floor, where, unlike the other levels, an actual bar dominated the loft space. Steel chairs and tables were crammed together for maximum occupancy.

Several members of her group chatted with one another. Karen sat in the dim corner, however, smiling at her friends but not quite engaging with them. He'd done this to her. Put her in a bad headspace such that she couldn't have fun with her peers. A few poorly chosen words had caused her to withdraw into herself, and he suspected her mind spun with so many thoughts, she couldn't both process them and be sociable.

He spun around and headed back downstairs. He'd just hit the first step when a finger tapped his shoulder. Karen's finger.

He held on to the stair rail and looked up at her.

"Going somewhere?" she asked with a soft smile.

"I didn't want to interrupt. Bad idea on my part." He gestured at his legs. "And I'm obviously not dressed to hang out."

She eyed his running outfit. "No, definitely not the suave businessman look I've come to know and love. Hang on. I could call it a night and come with you. Let me just get my purse."

She turned, but he tugged on her arm to stop her. "Karen. Stay."

She tilted her head to the side and squished her eyebrows together. "You don't want me to come home with you?"

"I'm headed out of town on business early tomorrow morning. A last-minute trip that couldn't be avoided."

"Oh, okay. When will you be back?"

"In about a week."

"Oh."

"It'll go by quickly. And when I get back, we'll have dinner. And talk. About us." He climbed the steps to reach the landing and kissed her on the forehead. "Take care of yourself."

He didn't look at her. Instead, he raced down the stairs and rushed out of the bar. The night air cooled his face as he gulped in air. Funny. He felt more winded now than he did after his run.

CHAPTER TWENTY-FIVE

Karen rushed down the main hall of the Fidler Building, eager to get to her human gross anatomy lecture. The entire first-year class of over two hundred students took the class, so getting a decent seat in the lecture hall proved to be a significant challenge.

She hovered near the door and scanned the room for a seat near the front. Pasha, a student in her study group, waved her over, pointing to the empty seat beside her.

"Hey, Pasha, thanks for saving me a seat," she said as she pulled her laptop from her backpack.

Pasha gave her a warm smile. "No problem."

During the first week of classes, she and Pasha had bonded over their mutual disdain for Henry Winslow, another student who'd weaseled his way into their study group. At their first meeting, Henry had claimed not to need a study group, explaining that he still wanted to join them because he thought the rest of the group might benefit from his input.

Pasha had wrapped her hands around her neck as though she

were being choked, and Karen had pretended to bang her head against the table, after which the women had shared conspiratorial smiles. Later, they'd entered into a pact to ignore Henry altogether.

"So today's the day, right?" she asked Pasha.

Pasha widened her eyes and nodded vigorously. "I hope we're in the same group. And I hope Henry gets booted off the island. I couldn't imagine having to be his lab partner."

The minute their professor entered the lecture hall, the boisterous chatter lowered to hushed whispers. Dressed in a lab jacket and gray slacks, with a pair of eyeglasses hanging from a silver chain around her neck, Professor Haines looked like she'd been plucked right out of central casting. She completed her professorial look with a perpetual scowl.

Their professor approached the podium and tapped on the mic. "Good morning, everyone. My teaching assistants will be posting the results of the first exam at the end of the class. Those of you who scored eighty percent or better will be e-mailed this afternoon with your lab group assignments and should report to the lab for the next class. The rest of you should report to the lecture hall. One of my TAs will be here to answer any questions. Bear in mind the retest will be a new set of questions. Okay, let's proceed with today's lecture."

At the end of the class, Karen sprinted to the back of the room and scanned the test results posted on the wall. The pages listed nothing but numbers: each student's personal identification number and their grade. She found her number and gasped: 58. *Shit*. Not only had she failed to make it into the first lab group but she'd bombed her first medical school exam, too. And if she didn't ace her remaining exams, she'd find herself on probation. Though tears threatened to fall, she blinked them away, smiling through the disappointment because Henry Winslow was staring at her.

"How'd you do?" he asked.

Henry knew asking that question was rude—the unwritten rule of med school was that people discussed grades only when that information was volunteered—but she was sure he didn't care. If an opportunity to gloat presented itself, the competitive jerk would take it.

Karen grimaced. "Didn't make it. Guess I'll be taking the retest in two weeks."

"Bummer," he said with a smile. "Better luck next time."

Still stunned by the exam result, she didn't bother to show her annoyance at Henry's obvious pleasure in her disappointing exam score. "Yeah. I've got some work to do."

Henry trotted away, an irritating spring in his step prompting her to picture him being attacked by a swarm of bees.

Pasha joined her, her face impassive.

Karen answered her silent question. "I didn't make it."

Pasha threw her hand around her shoulder. "I'm sorry, Karen. But you'll take the retest in two weeks and join us then. No big deal."

"Do you mind if I ask you how you did?"

Pasha hesitated. "Um. Ninety?"

Karen grinned. "Is that a question or an answer?"

Pasha blushed in response. "I scored a ninety," she said, this time with more confidence in her voice.

Pasha had two small children and a husband who worked irregular hours as a physician's assistant. How did *she* do it? "Congrats. That's fantastic. And I'm super impressed that you're able to keep your head on straight despite your personal responsibilities. What's your secret?"

Pasha covered her mouth and leaned in. "I totally ignore my kids and husband when I need to. In fact, it's a wonder my kids go to school with clothes on. And most days I make questionable fashion choices. I used to consider sending the kids to school with mismatched shoes a mistake. Now I've tricked them into thinking it's a style choice. There's no magic, Karen. It's all about priorities." Pasha paused. "My unsolicited advice? Don't get too caught up in that grade. It's your first exam. You'll rock the next one."

Karen nodded, mentally acknowledging what she'd been ignoring these past few weeks: She'd lost sight of her priorities. What medical student took a weekend trip to wine country just days before a major exam? Even her decision to hang out with her classmates at Bourbon had been out of character for her. The old Karen would have declined her classmates' invitation and spent the entire weekend studying instead. But she'd wanted to relax and get to know her classmates, something she'd never let herself do in college.

Karen had spent too much time with Mark and not enough time focused on her studies. But she would easily change that—because she had no other choice.

* * *

Mark rang the bell for Karen's apartment. He hadn't seen or heard from her for a week. They hadn't parted on the best terms the last time they'd seen each other at Bourbon so he wasn't surprised by her radio silence. Still, he wanted to check on her and make sure everything was okay.

Her soft voice crackled through the intercom. "Yes?"

"Karen, it's Mark."

She didn't respond.

"Karen?"

"Sorry. Let me buzz you in."

When he reached the second-floor landing, she stood at the threshold of her apartment, holding the door ajar. One bare foot covered the other, and dark circles rimmed her eyes. She looked so vulnerable standing there.

He wanted to hug her, but he placed his hands in his pockets instead. "Hey."

She swung open the apartment door and stepped aside to let him in. He followed her inside. She plopped onto the couch and gestured for him to take a seat, too. Books and papers covered her kitchen table, and a stack of dishes, one plate away from toppling over, sat in the sink. A pile of unfolded laundry partially hid the armchair in the far corner of the room.

"I haven't heard from you. I figured you were busy with classes, so I thought I'd give you some space."

"I appreciate that. And you're right. I've been slammed with work, so I haven't had a chance to call you. How have you been?"

He stared at her, trying to gauge her mood. "Is everything okay?"

"Everything's fine, Mark. I'm just busy. Every day can't be a fun fest. I assumed you of all people would understand. "

He chewed on his bottom lip and jammed his hands in his pockets. Busy was one thing, pissed off was quite another, and he couldn't shake the feeling that he was missing a critical piece of information. "Did something happen, Karen?"

Her cell phone rang before she could answer.

"Hello?" she said to the caller. "Oh, hey, Pasha." She rose from the couch and raised a single finger to let him know she'd need a minute.

He took the opportunity to survey her work space. Her anatomy book lay open on the table, and two stapled pages rested next to it with *58* written in red on the top sheet. She'd gotten a 58 on an exam. Mark sighed. It all made sense now. She'd gotten a poor grade, and she was upset about it. And given her distant demeanor, she blamed him for it, too.

What the hell was he doing messing around with her? She deserved better than this. She was embarking on a demanding journey to become a doctor. She didn't need him screwing with her head, and she deserved the freedom to do what she wanted, when she wanted, with whom she wanted. She needed to embrace these years, the ones in which she had no responsibility to anyone other than herself. So he would let her go. For her own good. And for his.

She ended the call and crossed the room, stopping a foot away from him. "Pasha's in my study group."

"And a friend?" he asked.

She furrowed her brows as though the idea were foreign to her. "Yes. Yes, I guess she is."

"Look, I came over to talk. I don't know how to say this…"

She stared at him, a resigned expression on her face. "Just say it, Mark."

"I think we should stop seeing each other."

CHAPTER TWENTY-SIX

Now there's a shocker."

Though she'd responded with sarcasm, she really was shocked. She'd spent the last few days trying to regroup, working through her concerns about their relationship and praying for a solution that wouldn't require her to end it. *A monumental waste of her time.* "Oh, I get it. All work and no fun makes Mark a very unhappy boy. Is that it?"

"That's not what this is about."

"It's not? Then what *is* this about? Because it seems to me that you're ready to bolt the minute we come close to acting like a normal couple, with everyday problems, and oh, I don't know, *issues.*"

Jaw clenched and nostrils flaring, he simply stood there, and as pathetic as it seemed, she was grateful even for that reaction. Without it, she would have seriously questioned whether he had any feelings for her at all.

When several tense seconds had passed, he spoke. "C'mon, Karen. What did you expect? That we'd ride off into the sunset together? You and I both know that was never going to happen."

"You know what I know? Against my better judgment, I gave us a chance, thinking that we might be able to meet in the middle. I could learn to loosen up a bit maybe, and you could learn to think of someone other than yourself for a change. I should have known that would be asking too much of you."

When he finally raised his head out of his proverbial ass, he refused to meet her gaze. But she didn't miss the glazed expression that passed over his face. His callous demeanor caused her stomach to twist. In that moment, she knew without a doubt that she'd been a temporary distraction for him.

Tears threatened to fall down her face, but she blinked several times to stem them. Three months ago, she'd been fine. Had a game plan for her future, and a singular purpose: to succeed in medical school. She'd let her relationship with him threaten her confidence. And because she had so little confidence in other areas of her life, the potential loss of that confidence—in the one aspect of her life where she'd excelled—shook her to the core. And for what? For a fling with someone who would never see her as anything but a plaything.

She glanced down at her hands and cursed them for shaking. Maintaining her composure had never seemed so important before. But despite her best efforts, her eyes watered. She gulped in air, but everything about her apartment stifled her. The dirty dishes in the sink. The pile of laundry judging her from its spot on her favorite armchair. The books strewn across her table. She needed to get her shit together.

She narrowed her eyes, her long lashes damp from the tears she hadn't been able to hold at bay. "You know, all this time, I've chastised myself for being weak, for worrying about what others think of me, for panicking in the face of situations that unnerved me. But you know what? I'm actually really strong. Unlike you, I confront my fears. You, on the other hand? You let your fears consume you."

He gritted his teeth and clenched his fists at his sides. "This isn't about me, Karen. Look, you're a young woman with so much ahead of her. We're not at the same place in our lives. You need to explore the possibilities. And I'm done with exploring. I did that ten years ago. I'm looking for something permanent."

When she titled her head to the side, he added, "*Eventually.*"

"Relationships don't come with blueprints, Mark. And you can't assume I'll do something simply because of my age. I'm not a fucking demographic. *I'm a person.* And why do you get to decide what's good for me?"

He raised his head to the ceiling in exasperation, and despite her nonviolent tendencies, she wanted to punch him in the throat.

"That's just it, Karen. I don't get to decide what's good for you. I get to decide what's good for me—and you're not it."

Her head snapped back as though he'd landed an upper cut to her chin. His words certainly had the same impact.

She groaned and squeezed her temples, finally accepting that she'd been drawn to him for superficial reasons. Tried to create substance where there was none. *What a fucking mess—and it was time to clean it up.* She wiped her tears and blew out a long breath. "This is the point in the conversation where I say I'm sorry."

* * *

Mark tried to catch up with the conversation. "Sorry?"

"Yes, sorry." Her voice quivered. "I got ahead of myself, and if I'd really been thinking, I would have figured out the problem sooner."

Disparate thoughts collided in his head. *What the hell was she talking about?* "I'm not sure I'm following you."

She raised her head to the ceiling and sighed. "Don't you see? Hero worship. I got so caught up in what you'd been able to draw out of me, I didn't realize I'd put you on a pedestal." She gave a bitter laugh. "As though you were the only man in the world who could bring me to satisfying orgasm. In romance books, it's called magic peen. When a woman thinks a man's penis is a wand capable of granting her every wish."

"That's what you think is going on here?"

"I do. And it was selfish of me to focus on my needs. As if you didn't have your own shit to work through. I blinded myself to it, or rather the magic peen blinded me to it. Meanwhile, you have issues, Mark. There's a reason you're a confirmed bachelor. There's a reason you'll never give yourself fully to any woman. Not even the woman you'll marry someday. So I'm really sorry if I put you in an uncomfortable position of having to deal with your issues *and* mine."

He stared at her, unable to digest how their relationship had deteriorated so quickly. A part of him wanted to apologize and tell her he'd do and be whatever she wanted. But the less selfish part of him knew he'd only be prolonging the inevitable demise of their relationship.

Nothing about her explanation made sense to him, but it gave him the out he needed. So he took it. "As I said, you're no good for me. And all that bullshit that just tumbled out of your mouth proves I'm not good for you, either." He threw open her apartment door. "I'll see you around, Karen."

CHAPTER TWENTY-SEVEN

In the two weeks after she and Mark parted ways, Karen buried herself in her work, filling every waking moment with tasks that would keep her mind busy. By design, she spared no time to think about him, and when she experienced a lull in her schedule, she read ahead in her classes to fill it.

In that time, Gracie had invited her to lunch, but she'd claimed to be too busy. Gracie being Gracie, she showed up at Karen's apartment unannounced on a Thursday evening.

"Karen, let me up," she said through the intercom.

Karen buzzed her in and waited for Gracie at the door. "Why didn't you call?"

Gracie responded as she climbed the last few steps. "Because I knew you wouldn't answer. And the last time you were this evasive, you were having a meltdown in college."

Karen followed her sister into the apartment and watched Gracie inspect the place. "I'm not having a meltdown." Truth. "I'm fine." Lie. "I've just been busy." Truth.

Gracie peered at her and shook her head. "You don't look fine. Come. Sit. Tell me what's going on."

So Karen told her about Mark, leaving out the sexy bits.

"I *knew* something was going on between you two. Ethan said I was crazy."

"You *knew*. How?"

Gracie rolled her eyes. "That embarrassing display at my apartment, that's how. Mimi knows, too. She only had a dozen photographs of her trip to Puerto Rico on that phone. The rest of the time, she'd been eavesdropping on you. You guys are amateurs. And thanks to you, I'll never look at flan the same way again." She shuddered for added effect. "Oh, and if I had any doubts, the fact that Mark never called Sharon was very telling."

"Yeah, well. He made very clear that I wasn't the right woman for him."

"And don't you think it's interesting that he completely rebuffed my efforts to set him up with a so-called *right* woman? He's scared, Karen."

"I know. But I'm the last person to tackle that issue with him. I have enough on my plate as it is."

Gracie reached over and squeezed Karen's hand. "Kar, I understand your desire to focus on school. I really do. But it is possible to be both a medical student and have a relationship. You wouldn't be breaking new ground here."

"I know it's *possible*, but it's not ideal."

"Who cares if it's ideal? And I think you're wrong about that anyway. Tell me this, have you ever considered that you could have a relationship with someone who would support you while you're in medical school? That having someone to lean on, or to get you through the tough times, might be a good thing."

Karen thought of Pasha, who managed her medical school career with two kids and a husband. She'd assumed Pasha excelled at school in spite of her family, but it occurred to her that it was possible, if not likely, that Pasha succeeded because of it. "I hear you, Gracie. I do."

Gracie threaded their hands together. "Just know that you don't have to do this alone."

But for the first time in her life, that's exactly how she felt: alone.

The next day, Professor Haines asked to see her after gross anatomy class,

"Ms. Ramirez, we haven't posted the results of the retake yet, but I just wanted to commend you on your performance. You received the highest score in the class."

Karen took a deep breath and smiled. "Thank you, Professor Haines. I don't think I've ever studied that much for an exam."

"Well, it showed. And perhaps your first score was just the kick in the pants you needed. I can tell by your comments and questions in class that you'll be an excellent student. Keep it up. We'll post the results tomorrow. You'll get your lab assignment then as well."

"Great. Thanks again."

Karen practically danced out of the lecture hall. Until she realized the practical effect of her grade on the exam: she was headed to the lab. A rite of passage for any first-year medical student, gross anatomy lab would require her to dissect a human cadaver. Haines expected the students to use a scalpel on a deceased person and speak coherently about the anatomical structures of that person's body.

Her lab group would "meet" the cadavers next week. Some students, she knew, would name them in an effort to humanize the experience; others would make crass jokes to hide their discomfort. Karen anticipated that she wouldn't even be able to enter the lab. And then what? She would fail the class, that's what. In fact, Karen questioned whether she'd ever be able to do it—and when she considered seeking someone's advice on how to handle it, only one person came to mind: Mark.

But she'd left him with the impression that she had only one use for him: to fulfill her physical needs. True, he hadn't believed her. While the notion had a certain surface appeal, she knew now that it was complete and utter bullshit, just as he'd suspected. She loved him. But he didn't want her love. Still, might they be able to move beyond their history and learn to be friends again? She hoped so, because she really needed him.

In a panic, she sat on her couch and picked up her cell. The desire to hear his voice was so great, her hands shook as she punched in his office number.

Expecting to hear his assistant's voice, her heart banged against her chest when he picked up on the second ring.

"This is Lansing."

Her voice, soft and raspy, savored the opportunity to speak his name. "Mark."

The silence stretched for more seconds than she could bear, so she filled it with her own voice. "Just listen, okay?"

He cleared his throat. "I'm listening."

"I don't think either one of us is free from blame here, but I wanted to say sorry for suggesting that you were nothing more to me than a warm body. You were much more to me than that. I can't pretend to understand your reasons for not wanting to work things out, but I respect your decision. More than anything, though, I realize I've lost a great deal by not having you as my friend."

"Thanks for saying that. And I apologize for my part in this. I'd like us to be friends, too."

"Okay."

"Okay."

Unable to remain in one place, she paced her living room. "Gross anatomy's not as bad as I thought it would be."

"Did Netter's book help?"

"Not really."

He laughed.

"I'm having a bit of a freak-out about meeting my first human cadaver next week."

"Damn. I'm not sure I could do that."

"I'm not sure I can do it, either."

"Afraid you're going to freeze up?"

This is what she missed: He understood her without her having to explain much at all. "Yeah."

"These cadavers. They're donated, right? By the deceased persons themselves, or by their families, right?"

"Yes."

"And presumably they donate them precisely so brilliant minds like yours can make a difference."

"Yes, I think so."

"So by cutting into that cadaver, you're granting their last wish for themselves. You and the cadaver are partners in this, if you will. Maybe if you thought about it like that, it would help."

The more she thought about it in that way, the more she warmed to the idea. "Yeah. You might be on to something. Thanks."

"Good luck next week. I'll be sending you good vibes, and I know you'll be great."

"Thanks, Mark."

"Take care, Karen."

He'd never doubted her ability to succeed, not once. She needed a friend like him in her life. And if her heart broke a little knowing what might have been, she'd get over it. Eventually.

* * *

Mark's hand shook as he placed the receiver in its cradle. Hearing Karen's voice had floored him. He imagined seeing her in person would be twice as hard.

Running a hand through his hair, he stood and paced his office, the room suddenly too small for the thoughts bouncing around in his head. He'd done the right thing by pushing her away, but knowing that didn't make him miss her any less.

His gaze landed on his chair, and he pictured Karen's as she straddled him in that very spot. Dammit. What he needed was to get away from the office. And he needed to check on his father, who wasn't returning his calls.

He hit the intercom. "Nicole, please cancel my afternoon appointments."

Two hours later, Mark arrived at his father's home on Kent Island. The modest cottage was situated on the waterfront. What it lacked in amenities it more than made up for with its gorgeous views. Mark walked onto the screened front porch and found the front door unlocked. "Dad?"

Nothing.

"Dad? Where are you?"

Mark wandered the halls. The hardwoods gleamed, and fresh flowers sat on the kitchen counter. His father had even drawn the curtains in the living room, letting the natural sunlight in. His father rarely paid attention to such niceties. Each of these changes must have resulted from his mother's influence.

Mark peeked into the kitchen alcove, expecting to see his father sipping a cup of coffee, but he wasn't there, either. He did find him sitting by the bay window in his bedroom, however, a closed book in his hand.

"Hey, Dad."

His father didn't turn around. He simply stroked the spine of the book and stared out the window. "Hey, son."

"Everything okay?"

"Everything's fine."

Mark stepped into the room and sat on the edge of his father's bed. "I've been calling and couldn't reach you. Thought I'd check to make sure you were alive."

His father didn't laugh as Mark had expected.

"Sorry. I've been preoccupied. Haven't been checking my phone."

Now he got it. Paul often went off the grid when he was working on a journal article. Had Mark been thinking clearly, he would have realized this was one of those times. "The place has Lisa's touch. It's nice. Was she here this weekend?"

"She was, but she won't be coming back."

The statement sucked the air out of him. He'd heard a version of that phrase before, more than two decades ago, in fact, and its impact was no less devastating today than it had been then. But this time he hurt for his father. "What happened, Dad?"

"She's decided to go back to that man…her ex-husband."

"Richard."

"Right. Richard."

"I take it you had no choice in the matter."

His father looked over his shoulder. "Bingo."

Mark rose from the bed and placed a hand on his father's shoulder. "I'm sorry."

"I'm sorry, too."

Mark cocked his head back. Maybe he'd misheard his father. "Sorry? What are you sorry for?"

"I'm sorry for falling in love with such a selfish woman. She's never put anyone first in her life but herself. All these years I've blamed myself for her decision to leave. Told myself I had no business trying to stifle someone so young, so unsure of who she wanted to be. But your mother will never change. She leaves because she wants to, because it's always been about her. Our needs never figured into the equation."

The weariness in his father's voice made Mark want to throw something. All these years, he'd assumed his father had picked the wrong kind of person: too young and unsettled to know what she wanted. He realized now he'd been wrong on too many levels to count. His mother hadn't been the wrong kind of person for his father; she'd simply been the wrong person for anyone. Because what mattered to her always came first. And it struck him then that he and his father had settled into the shadows of their mother's desertion, letting it define them rather than letting it define *her*.

He pictured Karen's tear-streaked face as she accused him of discounting their relationship because of what he predicted she would do, of pushing her away to protect himself. Her assessment had been dead-on.

He laid a hand on his father's shoulder. "Dad, we're going to be okay. We're better off without her."

And it hit him then: He wasn't better off without Karen, though. Which raised the important question: What was he willing to do about it?

CHAPTER TWENTY-EIGHT

Professor Haines had paired Karen with three male students, and their cadaver was a woman. This didn't bode well. Each student wore blue scrubs, and although the professor had stressed that there would be no dissections today, the med school had provided aprons as another layer of protection.

The lab was surprisingly bright. She surveyed the room and the faces of her colleagues, some of whom looked pale, others of whom cracked jokes. She could see that other students were uncomfortable, too.

Karen stood outside the group, ready to bolt. Her skin itched as though thousands of ants had burrowed under her skin. She didn't dare scratch herself, not in here. The air was stale, but it had no stench to it. Nonetheless, Karen breathed through her mouth, in part because the steady inhale and exhale calmed her.

Various teaching assistants wheeled out the gurneys. Professor Haines addressed the group. "This class will run through the spring, and I've allotted plenty of time to ease you into the practice of working with cadavers. If you need a break or a moment to collect yourself, please take it. I'd much prefer for you to leave the lab than pass out in here."

A few students laughed. Professor Haines did not. "I'm not kidding."

Karen didn't need to be told twice. She might be labeled a wuss, but she didn't care. Her sense of self-preservation propelled her out the door.

Outside the lab, a small atrium provided elevated bench seating. Karen collapsed on one of the wooden benches and dropped her head between her legs. She breathed in and out. She had to conquer this.

The bench next to hers creaked, and she sat up. Eyes blinking furiously, she gasped. "What are you doing here?"

Mark stood and pulled her out of her seat. "I thought you might need a friend today."

She threw her arms around him and squeezed him as hard as she could. "I do. I really, really do."

"I'm here."

She backed away and examined his face. His chiseled features hadn't changed, but his brown eyes, which had been so cold the last time they'd seen each other, now shone warm and bright. "It's good to see you."

"Can I take you to lunch when you're done?"

She hesitated.

He supplied the missing pieces. "To talk. About us."

"Sure. Assuming I don't pass out, I'll be done in an hour."

He nodded and pointed to the newspaper and smartphone in his hand. "I'll wait. Remember, there isn't anything you can't do if you want it badly enough. I have one hundred percent confidence in you." Several students walked back into the lab. He watched them until they disappeared, and then he smiled at her. "You ready?"

She returned his smile. "I'm ready."

An hour later, she emerged from the lab, swinging her arms as she walked toward Mark. "Done."

He stood and led her to the exit. "How'd it go?"

"It went well. I didn't pass out."

"I'm proud of you."

"I'm proud of me, too."

* * *

"We're having lunch in your condo?" she asked as she undid her seat belt.

"Yes. My personal chef left us a feast. She even learned how to make an empanada for you."

"Wow. I'm impressed and honored."

Which meant what? He'd planned this excursion? For her?

Mark was uncharacteristically quiet as they rode the elevator, his only movement an incessant tapping of the newspaper against his thigh. When they reached his floor, he ushered her through the door and turned to her. "Check it out."

Karen walked into the large space, which wasn't quite as wide open as it had been before. He'd added plants to the place, the pop of green a welcome addition to the slate gray and white palette. Oh, and a lovely multicolored painting of a dancer hung on the main wall. "You added color."

"That's right. You said that's what you'd do, remember?"

Karen nodded slowly. "I remember. What's happening over there?"

Part of the loft had been converted to a construction zone, complete with scaffolding and dusty drop cloths.

"I'm building an office."

"I thought you didn't want an office. You said you didn't want to bring work home."

Mark rubbed the back of his neck and stared at a spot behind her. "I still don't. The office is for you."

Karen couldn't process what he was saying. The office was for her? She lifted his chin until he looked at her. "Mark, what is all this?"

"Let me back up a minute. I need to explain why I acted like an ass when I was in your apartment."

"Okay."

"My mother and father rekindled their relationship a few weeks ago."

She smiled. "Mark, that's great."

He shook his head. "No, it isn't. She left again."

She grabbed his hands and squeezed them. "I'm sorry."

"It made me realize I'd fought my feelings for you because I didn't want to find myself in the same situation as my father. But my mother is my mother. And you're you. I convinced myself that breaking up with you was in your best interests, but really, I was scared." He wrapped her in his arms, embracing her tightly. "And I realized that if I didn't face my fears, I'd lose you. I *love you*. And I don't want to fight it anymore."

Her eyes watered, and her vision blurred. "I can't believe you're saying this."

"Believe it." To prove his point, he threaded his fingers through the hair at her temples and swooped down for a kiss. Karen pressed into him, wanting her entire body connected to his. He licked his way inside her mouth, and she opened to him fully.

God, she'd missed this.

Finally, they moved apart.

He pinned her with his heavy gaze. "The day you called me at the office. I loved that you called, but I hated that we were having that conversation by telephone."

She knew exactly what he meant, because she'd felt the same way.

He tucked a strand of her hair behind her ear. "I want to be the one you talk to when something's bothering you, just as I'd want you to be that person for me. But I want to be able to turn on my side in bed and talk to you, our faces inches apart. Or I want you to stop in the office unannounced and have every right to be there. I want you with me. Period. And if you need space, I'll give it to you. I'll need mine, too. But at the end of the day, you're the one I want to come home to. I love you, Karen."

Those words wrapped around her like the coziest blanket imaginable, leaving her safe and protected. "I love you, too, Mark. So much. And I want all that, too, but can we take it slowly?"

He raised a single eyebrow, a smug smile suggesting he thought the idea was preposterous.

"I tell you what. As soon as you move in with me, you can take all the time you need."

She smirked. "You're very persuasive, Mr. Lansing."

He gave her a quick kiss on the lips. "You think so? There's more where that came from."

She grinned at him. "What you got? Impress me."

"If you move in with me, I'll let you play with my anatomy all night."

She returned his quick kiss. "Sold."

"One more thing," he said as he folded her in his arms. "I got the swing."

She stepped back. "You didn't."

"Oh, I assure you, Karen, I did. It's in the bedroom." He gave her a suggestive smile. "Want to see it?"

"Very subtle, Mr. Lansing. Very subtle."

About the Author

Mia Sosa was born and raised in New York. She attended the University of Pennsylvania, where she earned her bachelor's degree in communications and met her own romantic hero, her husband. She once dreamed of being a professional singer, but then she discovered she would have to perform onstage to realize that dream and decided to take the law school admissions test instead. A graduate of Yale Law School, Mia practiced First Amendment and media law in the nation's capital for ten years before returning to her creative roots. Now, she spends most of her days writing contemporary romances about smart women and the complicated men who love them. Okay, let's be real here: She wears PJs all day and watches more reality television than a network television censor—all in the name of research, of course. Mia lives in Maryland with her husband and two daughters and is still on the hunt for the perfect karaoke bar.

Learn more at:

www.MiaSosa.com

Twitter: @MiaSosaRomance

Facebook.com/miasosa.author

Did you miss Gracie and Ethan's love story?

Please see the next page for an excerpt from the first book in Mia Sosa's The Suits Undone series, *Unbuttoning the CEO*!

CHAPTER ONE

Ethan Hill couldn't have imagined a more craptastic morning.

He stood next to his lawyer in a dim and musty courtroom in the nation's capital. The dreary atmosphere made his stomach churn. And the gluten-free muffin his assistant had given him earlier wasn't helping matters. Now that he thought about it, what the hell was wrong with gluten anyway?

Judge Monroe, a regal woman with a crop of silver hair and flawless skin, peered at him over her tortoiseshell-framed glasses and cleared her throat. "Mr. Hill, as I'm sure you're aware, a reckless driving conviction carries the possibility of a one-year jail sentence. It's not my penalty of choice, but given that you've accumulated five speeding tickets in as many months, a fine won't do."

Jail? Was she seriously considering jail? Ethan's heart raced, and his knees threatened to buckle. He even considered running through the Lamaze breathing his sister Emily had practiced in preparation for the birth of his niece. *Hee-hee-hooo. Hee-hee-hooo.*

Judge Monroe clasped her hands and leaned forward. "Your company's support of charities is to be commended. But in my view, a man who claims such *devotion* to charitable endeavors ought to spend time serving the community rather than throwing money at it. I'm sentencing you to community service."

Ethan's heart slowed to a gallop. Given a choice between jail and a couple of weeks of community service, he'd pick community service any day. "Thank you, Judge Monroe."

"Hold on, Mr. Hill. You might not want to thank me just yet."

Ethan's stomach twisted, ending its protest with a loud gurgle. *Damn you, gluten-free muffin.*

Judge Monroe scribbled on a legal pad. Ethan couldn't see what she wrote, but the hard strokes of her pen suggested she wanted to stick a figurative foot up his butt. Ethan mentally prepared himself to bend over.

After a few seconds, the judge looked up and smirked. Or was that a snort? Dammit, he wasn't sure.

"Mr. Hill, I'm sentencing you to two hundred hours of community service, to be completed with one charitable organization over the course of the next six months. Choose a charity that could benefit from your technical skills. And have your lawyer inform my clerk of the charity you've selected."

Ethan swiped a hand down his face. The sentence was outrageous. He calculated the hours in his head, figuring he'd have to spend just under eight hours a week for the next twenty-six weeks to fulfill the sentence. He doubted he could manage to do that on top of his eighty-hour workweek, but he didn't appear to have a choice.

His lawyer, a buddy from college with stellar credentials and a ruddy, cherubic face, leaned his stocky frame toward Ethan and whispered in his ear. "You got off easy, pal. Judge Monroe tends to take creativity to a new level when she's pissed. She must have gotten laid last night."

Ethan's gaze darted to the judge, whose tight expression made him wonder whether she'd heard his lawyer's quip. He'd dealt with intimidating businessmen twice her size, but when her bespectacled gaze landed on his face, Ethan barely suppressed the urge to squirm.

She took a deep breath. "Mr. Hill, use this sentence as an opportunity to think about your choices. Self-destructive behavior is one thing. Behavior that endangers others is quite another. And be prepared to take the bus for the next several months. What you do after that is up to you, but if you get another speeding ticket, this court will impose the maximum penalty. Got it?"

"Got it, Your Honor."

Judge Monroe nodded. "Court is adjourned."

The slam of her gavel against the bench might as well have been a slap upside his head. As he watched the judge exit the courtroom, Ethan vowed never to speed again. He couldn't afford to go to jail. Not again anyway.

* * *

Back at the office, Ethan's first task was to update the company's board about his legal situation. Two years ago, the board had taken a chance on him. He'd be wise not to alienate any of its members, especially when those members had hired him based on his vow that his reckless days were over.

He'd just begun to type an e-mail to the board when Mark Lansing, the company's CFO, waltzed into his office. Mark also served as his personal pain in the ass. And though he hesitated to tell Mark this, Ethan considered the man his best friend.

"Well, well," Mark said. "If it isn't Dale Earnhardt, Jr., in the flesh."

"Very funny. This time, I'm screwed."

Mark rubbed his hands together as he sat down. He didn't bother to hide his wide grin. "What happened?"

"She gave me community service. Two hundred hours of it."

Mark scrunched his brows and whistled. "That's harsh."

"Harsh or not, the sentence stands."

"How long do you have?"

"Six months. I get to pick the organization, but it has to be the right fit for my technical skills, whatever that means. And I'm going to use my first name there."

He hadn't used his first name since he'd left home to attend college at Penn. Sure, he wasn't a household name, but thanks to Google, anyone could easily discover his role in the corporation. If all went according to plan, no one at the organization would know he was the CEO of a multimillion-dollar communications company. And no one would know about his unflattering past. *How refreshing.*

Mark tapped his lips with a single finger. "And by first name, do you mean you plan to go in under the radar?"

Exactly. If no one knew who he was, the board could pretend it never happened. "Right. Something on your mind, Mark?"

Mark's gaze shifted around the room as he tapped his hands on Ethan's desk. His eyes were bright. Too bright. "Give me a minute. I'll be right back." Before Ethan could stop him, Mark shot out of the chair and left the office.

Ethan turned back to his computer. He'd just finished the e-mail to the board when Mark returned and dropped a section of the day's newspaper on his desk.

"Check that out," Mark said.

Ethan sighed, the steady throb at his temples making him more irritable than usual. "What am I looking for?"

"C-2. Flip the page."

Ethan turned the page. The headline of the full-page article read, LEARN TO NET TEACHES STUDENTS AND SENIORS HOW TO SURF THE WEB.

A photograph of a woman and two young boys accompanied the article. The boys sat in front of a computer and the woman stood behind them, her arms draped over their shoulders. Her dark, wavy hair fell against her cheeks, and her brown eyes gleamed with excitement. He scanned the first paragraph, searching for her name.

Graciela Ramirez.

A dozen images hit him at once. All of them involved Ms. Ramirez in a compromising position. With him. He looked up at Mark, who studied his reaction to the photograph. Ethan shrugged and tossed the newspaper on the ever-increasing pile of untouched papers on his desk. "I'll read it later. I need to get this e-mail out to the board."

Mark smirked. "Okay, sure. It's too bad, though."

"What's too bad?"

"She's engaged."

If he'd had a gun pointed to his head, Ethan would have been hard-pressed to explain why he was disappointed by that knowledge. "How do you know?"

Mark smiled. "It says so in the article you're going to read as soon as I leave." With his smile still in place, Mark sauntered through the door and saluted Ethan before he closed it.

When the door clicked shut, Ethan dove for the paper and placed the page in front of him. According to the article, Ms. Ramirez had been promoted from program manager to director three months ago.

The mission of Learn to Net—or LTN, as she referred to it in the article—was to serve individuals without regular access to computers, educating them about online research libraries, online job applications, social media websites, and other resources on the Web.

He read further, looking for information about Ms. Ramirez's engagement. Finding none, he gritted his teeth, speed-dialed Mark, and placed the phone in speaker mode.

Mark answered after the first ring. "What?"

"It doesn't say she's engaged."

Mark chuckled. "No, it doesn't. But you'd only know that if you read the entire article in the few minutes since I left your office. You're so predictable that I can predict when you're trying not to be predictable."

"Is she engaged or not?"

"I have no clue," Mark said.

"Do you know anything else about her?"

"Nope."

Ethan threw his head back against his chair. "I'm surrounded by people who are useless to me."

"You're wrong. I listen. Aren't you the man who whined about wanting to meet someone without the baggage of your pseudo-celebrity status getting in the way? Here's your chance, *Nic.*"

"Your craftiness scares even me."

Mark snorted. "One day, you'll thank me. I'm hanging up now."

"No, wait."

"Is this about the company?" Mark asked.

"Yes."

"Good, because I'm not inclined to provide any more advice about your miserable love life."

"Mark, shut the hell up already. This is about the computer systems upgrade."

"What about it?"

"Where are the old computers going?"

"I don't know. The IT department handles recycling and donations."

"Have the old computers donated to Learn to Net, but arrange for them to be donated anonymously."

"I'd love to, but I can't."

"Why not?"

"No low-key donations, remember? Board policy. All charitable donations are to be publicized within an inch of their lives. The gift of corporate giving comes with shameless promotion of the company."

Of course. Ethan had recommended that policy. From a business perspective, it made sense. Now, it seemed cold. Manipulative. "I remember. Never mind."

"Anything else?"

"No, that's all," Ethan said. Then he disconnected the call.

Rather than e-mail the board, Ethan browsed LTN's website. It was a legitimate charitable organization, with locations in New York and D.C. Given his company's interests in Internet communications, Ethan's decision to complete his community service hours with the organization was a no-brainer. His choice to serve there had nothing to do with its director. *Yeah. Right.*

Ethan squeezed his stress ball, a constant companion since he'd become the company's CEO. He hoped he wouldn't regret the decision to work with LTN. The court had ordered him to serve the community. And he would. Pretending to be someone else. At an organization with an attractive woman at its helm. *What could go wrong?*

* * *

Gracie Ramirez sat at her desk and reread the letter she'd received from Nathan Dempsey, a lawyer at a prestigious law firm near DuPont Circle. Two weeks ago, she'd agreed to host a man who'd been sentenced to community service for reckless driving. Nicholas E. Hill. Sounded plain enough. Mr. Hill's lawyer had assured her that his client posed no threat to her or LTN's members, and he'd even provided a statement attesting to Mr. Hill's criminal record. According to that record, the man only possessed a lead foot, but given LTN's limited resources, she would have been crazy not to accept the free help that went along with that foot.

With her morning to-do list set, she turned to her computer to work on LTN's annual report. Her fingers hovered over the keyboard, however, and she dropped her head. She had yet to tackle the worst part—the organization's woeful lack of funding.

Uh-uh. There'd be no pity party for her. She was going to stay positive. She refused to dwell on the fact that she'd inherited a mess of an organization, one that hadn't made a serious effort to solicit donations to ensure a steady cash flow. Still, if she didn't secure funding soon, the doors of the D.C. location would close by the end of the fiscal year. And Gracie would return to New York, where her father would greet her with open arms and a smug expression.

She'd accepted failure in her love life, but failure in her professional life was *not* an option.

A rap on her door jolted her out of her thoughts. Gracie grimaced when she saw Daniel Vargas standing at the threshold. His family, like hers, lived in New York. Somehow he'd finagled his way onto LTN's board. As a result, she'd come to think of him as her father's spy.

Daniel swept into her office and assumed a stance that reminded her of a soldier at attention: feet wide apart, chest out, and hands behind his back. "*Hola, Graciela, esta todo bien?*"

"At ease, Mr. Vargas. Everything's fine. What can I do for you?"

"I was wondering if you're available for lunch."

Gracie was thankful she had a good excuse today to turn him down. "I can't, Daniel. I have someone coming in soon. For community service. I have to give him a tour of the facility and get him started on a couple of projects."

"Fine. Another time, then."

Daniel was a prominent architect in the city, and almost universally regarded as a catch. Daniel himself thought he was a catch. Just another reason she considered him an arrogant and eligible man who simply happened to draw excellent architectural plans.

Gracie opened a drawer and reached for her purse, an excuse to avoid his gaze as she turned him down for the fifth time. "Daniel, we've been over this before. It's not going to happen. I just don't think of you that way. And your role on the board presents a clear conflict of interest." She peeked at him to gauge whether any of her spiel was sinking in.

His chest caved in at her words, but then it puffed back out. "I'm a patient man, Graciela. You will come to your senses. And when you do, I'll resign from the board. It's that easy."

Gracie's mouth gaped. Did he think the casual way in which he treated his position on the board somehow endeared him to her? Not in this lifetime. "I've got a lot of work to do, Daniel. Was there anything else?"

Wise enough to take the hint, he cut a corner and pivoted toward the door. "No, no. I'll catch up with you some other time."

She waved him off, dismissing him and his perfectly styled hair.

With Daniel gone, she swiveled her chair toward her computer screen and returned to the annual report. Thirty minutes later, her office phone buzzed and the voice of her assistant, Brenda, filled the room. "Gracie, Nicholas Hill is here to see you." After that announcement, Brenda's voice lowered to a whisper. "He's hot, Gracie. I think I'm going to head to the bathroom to sort myself out."

Gracie rolled her eyes. Brenda was a smart and efficient assistant, but she had either no ability or no desire to filter her inappropriate thoughts, which meant she shared them with Gracie—often.

"I'll be right out," Gracie said.

She straightened in her chair and twisted her neck from side to side to ease the tightness in her shoulders. Checking her reflection in the mirror near her door, she licked her lips and swept her hair away from her face. Before she reached the reception area, she took a deep breath and pasted on a welcoming smile.

Brenda came into view first. Gracie resisted the urge to laugh when her assistant fanned herself. *Focus, Gracie. Focus.*

Nicholas Hill stood with his back to her, giving Gracie a few seconds to glance at her feet to be sure her hem wasn't tucked into a shoe. Distracted by her wardrobe check, she gave him her typical perfunctory greeting as she held out her hand. "Welcome, Mr. Hill. My name is Graciela Ramirez, the director of Learn to Net. Call me Gracie. It's a pleasure to meet—"

When Nicholas Hill's warm hand grasped hers, she looked up at him and her mouth stopped moving. Brenda's assessment of his appearance was trite, but Gracie had to admit the description was spot on. This man—*her ward for two hundred hours*—rendered her speechless.

Taking in the twinkle in his green eyes and the lopsided grin that emphasized his full lips, Gracie wanted to stuff him in a box, slap a bow on it, and set it under the Christmas tree. What the hell? So unlike her. And unsettling. Frankly, she needed a minute to collect herself, because he was too much to absorb at once.

"Hello, Gracie. This isn't the best of circumstances, but it's a pleasure to meet you. And call me . . ." He paused. "Call me Nic."

Nic's deep voice filled the space as his fingers lingered on hers. Her gaze dropped to their clasped hands, a joining more intimate than it should have been in this context. He snatched his hand away, maybe in recognition of that fact, and ran it through his tousled, dark brown hair. Gracie's fingers itched to touch those locks, because she knew they'd be just as soft as they promised. Returning her gaze to his face, she suppressed a sigh.

Wait. She had to remember why he was here. He was a reckless driver, and that was a bad thing. *Bad, bad, bad.* But she couldn't help wondering whether he was reckless in more pleasurable ways. *Yum, yum, yum.*

Ugh. Get it together, Gracie. He's just a man, and you're a smart, capable professional who has an important nonprofit to run, she reminded herself.

She cleared her throat and willed herself to settle down. "I'll show you around and then we can head back to my office to discuss the projects I'd like your help with. Sound good?"

"Sounds great," he said. "Lead the way."

Gracie hesitated. It was a truth universally acknowledged that a man in possession of a pair of eyes would check out a woman's butt upon meeting her. Hoping to divert him from checking out said butt, she walked beside him and pointed out the framed awards that hung on the walls.

She was sure he was no stranger to women who came undone in his presence, and she didn't want to be the latest poor soul to join them. She tried. She did. But when she closed her eyes for the briefest of moments, she imagined Nic's lips pressed against her neck as he held her in his arms. *Do not think of him in that way. Do not think of him in that way.*

Saving LTN was her highest priority. She couldn't afford to be distracted by any man. So it should have been no surprise that Nic was distraction personified. Somewhere the gods were laughing at her. Six months. She could ignore him for that long, right? *Right.*